Indigo

I don't know if any of this is good or bad.
All I know is whatever it is—**I can't stop it.**

AMBER LACIE

69,200 words

Cover Art by Bookend Design

Editing and Formatting by Gray Publishing Services

ISBN 978-1973892328

Dedication

For Lindsey, my partner in crime, you are my very best friend. Thank you for being my person. I love you, sister.

To that one person, thievery is not a form of flattery.

CONTENTS

Visit Amber Lacie's website for the latest news and updates.

Website: http://www.amberlacieauthor.wix.com/author-blog

Twitter: @amber_lacie

Facebook: www.facebook.com/amberlacieauthor

Acknowledgments

Writing a book is no small feat. There are so many people who help me along the way. I want to say thank you to all of my readers who have supported me along the way. Your encouragement and love of the written word is what keeps me pushing forward.

There are a select few who read my words in their raw state, well before the editing or formatting takes place. They help me smooth the flow of the story, as well as build the characters you will find within these pages.

Thank you, Angie & Jen, for always being supportive. I flove you both. (To those that may question my spelling, flove is spelled correctly.)

To my husband who makes me laugh daily, thank you so much for inspiring the laughter in these pages. I love you.

To my kids, I love you. Be nice to each other—always gentle and always kind.

Prologue

LEX

My flight to California leaves at noon tomorrow. I love spending time with the family, but I've waited my whole life for this chance. Twenty-two years may not seem like a long time, but to me—it is. Since I was four years old and could wrap my head around the game of baseball, I knew it was what I was going to do with my life. I eat, sleep, and breathe the sport, so when University of Southern California offered me a scholarship—I jumped on it. There was no way I was passing up that opportunity. It was one of the best decisions I ever made. With college being behind me, I'm going to be able to pursue my love for baseball for years. I'm getting called up to the majors.

My agent called me last night and said it was a done deal, so tomorrow afternoon I will be signing a contract with the big boys. I was lucky enough to catch some time off before training started so I packed up my car and headed home. There's no sense in keeping my car with me while I hop from place to place, so until I find my own pad, my brother is going to keep an eye on her for me. Yeah, my car is a she. She's too sexy not to be.

Today is my last day at home in Alabama, and I'm about to make the best of it. I raked my fingers through my ash brown hair before slipping my baseball cap on. Squinting my eyes in the afternoon sun, I eyed the pavement around me. It stopped raining hours ago, but I could still see a couple of wet spots on the driveway. *There's no way the sun can absorb any more water today—not in this humidity.* The air was so wet, I'm sure if I turned around fast enough, I'd be able to catch a cloud in my hands.

Rain or no rain; there was nothing that would stop me from finally showing my dad what she's got. I ran my fingers across the deep plum purple paint as my hand slid over the hood of my 1969 Dodge Charger. It took me a while to find a body shop in Southern California that could finish her just the way I wanted, but it was worth the wait——and the cash. Her body is sick, and the sound she makes when she roars to life flashes goosebumps across my skin. I still remember the day I picked her up.

They had her covered with a light brown tarp. Julio pulled it off, revealing the sweetest car I'd ever seen. I had to reach down to adjust my jeans because I was getting a hard-on. It might seem like a weird reaction, but I couldn't help it. This car was made for me, and my cock knew what it was going to be like to feel that kind of power under my control. Julio must have caught my reaction because his head tipped back with a rich laugh falling from his lips. He tossed me the keys and I clapped him on the back before jumping into my new baby.

It took me a few minutes to adjust the mirrors and my seat to fit my long legs. Julio had it set to fit him, but my six-foot two-inch frame doesn't fit well in spaces adjusted to fit someone who's only five-foot seven. Taking a deep breath, I stretched my arms out in front of me before sliding the key into the ignition, which would bring the sexy beast to life. She roared at the turn of the key. The purring I felt underneath me didn't do anything to help ease the strain of my hard cock pressed against my jeans. Slamming on the gas, I peeled out of the garage leaving a laughing Julio behind me.

Fuck, I loved feeling her grip the pavement. Damn, I have a hard-on just thinking about it. Pulled from my thoughts by the sound of my dad's voice calling out for me, I quickly adjusted myself.

"Lex—you out here, boy?"

Turning around, I leaned against my baby. "Yeah, I'm out here, dad. Y'all ready to go?"

"Yeah. Your momma is coming too."

My dad isn't a big man; I easily tower over him, though no one is sure where my height comes from, since both of my parents seem to be vertically challenged. My dad swears I got it from his side, because his side of the family was built to work. I'm not sure what to take from that, but that's what I've been told most of my life.

A grin slid across my face seeing my older brother walk out with my mom right behind him. *Hell yeah. I can't wait to get her on the road.*

My brother, Logan, was one of the best mechanics around. He has always loved rebuilding forgotten dreams. In fact, he helped me find this beauty when I was still in high school. He also helped me get her up and running before I left for college. I worked two jobs while going to school full time so I could pay Julio to finish the job. This was my chance to show her off.

Jumping into the driver's seat, I waited for them to finish arguing about who was riding bitch. We all knew it would be my mom, but we wouldn't be us if we didn't give her a hard time about it. We're her boys. We always give her a hard time—it's what we do. I waited for the click of the last seatbelt before throwing her into gear. She screamed across the pavement as the tires squealed beneath us.

"Lex."

They were the only words that fell from my mom's lips. I instantly let off the gas and turned onto the main road, which went through town. I knew better than to show off in front of her, but I had to. I had to do it this once.

By going through town I was only able to get her up to about thirty-five miles per hour. *She can do better than this.* Glancing over to my mom, I made sure to let my bottom lip stick out just a bit. I'm the baby in the family, and she's always had a hard time telling me no. Rolling her eyes she gave me a small nod of her head. Turning off the main road, I followed the back roads between the farms. Some of the curves were steep, but I knew she could handle it, so my foot pressed on the gas a little harder.

Logan was in the back seat yelling up a storm. He was loving every minute of it. My dad was laughing, while my mom was nervously gripping her seat. As I got closer to the Tennessee state line the roads got a little steeper. Normally I would slow down, but I was having too much fun. As a truck passed us from the other direction, it sprayed mist up onto the windshield with its tires, and my wipers effortlessly flicked it away.

I should slow down.

As soon as I noticed the water kicking up from his tires, I should have slowed down, but I didn't. I was a God and nothing could stop me.

Taking the curve to the right, I could feel my tires slip a bit. My mom screamed my name and I reassured her that I had it—but I didn't. Gripping my wheel, I jerked it hard to the left, and the back end of the car slammed against the rock wall to my right, causing us to spin out.

Everything moved slowly at first. I could see the crack in the windshield slowly spread like a lightning bolt reaching across an open field. Feeling us spin out of control, the car flipped over and we slammed against the hard ground, but we didn't stop. The metal around us bent and twisted as it fell down the small ravine. My body jerked forward as we slammed into something hard and unmoving. I heard someone calling my name, but it took me a few minutes to gather my bearings.

Hanging upside down from my seat, I pressed my hand against the ceiling to brace myself, before unbuckling my seatbelt. My shoulder slammed into the ceiling, but the car didn't budge. Turning my head, I could see my mom. Blood and glass were everywhere, and a thick branch, maybe it was a limb, I'm not sure, was pinning her against the seat. Gently brushing her hair out of her face, I called her name. At least I think I called her name. I'm not actually sure if any words were falling from my lips. Blood was coming from her ears and her nose. Doing my best to lean across her, I gently pressed my fingers against her neck. Vacant, lifeless, blue eyes looked back at me.

My stomach twisted as my heart carved into itself with a steel blade. *What. The. Fuck. Have. I. Done?*

"Lex?" I heard my name again. Shifting my body so I can turn slightly, I saw my dad behind me, hanging from his seat. I reached for him but he shook his head no. "Logan—Logan first." I nodded my head at his choked words. Kicking at my door, I was able to break my window, giving me just enough room to crawl out against the twisted branches. My feet hung a foot or two off the ground as my body slid from the wreckage. Letting go, my body crumbled beneath me as a burning sensation raced up my right leg.

I tried my dad's door first, despite his plea for Logan, but it wouldn't budge. Pain ricocheted through my body as I made my way around the back of the car to Logan's door. The metal was twisted, jamming the door shut. Seeing Logan's head hanging, I yelled for him to cover his face. I'm not sure if he heard me, but his body didn't move. Using a rock I found on the ground, I broke his window, giving me access to him. Crawling through the window, scraping my stomach against the broken glass, my fingers stretched out in front of me, unlatching the seatbelt holding his body in place. His shoulders and neck slammed against the roof of the car as he fell from his restraints.

Slipping my arms under his shoulders, I turned him slightly to the left and dragged his body out of the window. I was able to pull him away from the car, about fifteen feet or so, before my legs gave out on me. Checking for signs of life, I found that Logan was breathing, but I couldn't get him to respond. Leaving him lying against the side of the ravine, I crawled back toward the car, as the pain in my leg wouldn't allow me to stand anymore. I tried, but my leg buckled under the weight of my body.

Hearing the sound of a loud snap, my head jerked back toward the car just in time to see the tree break that was holding it in place. The car slid a few more feet before becoming lodged between the bottom of the steep incline and the rocks at my feet. I could see liquid running down the windows but I couldn't figure out what it was. Yelling out for my dad, he didn't move. Slamming my fists against the window, my strength was no match for the glass; it didn't even splinter from my abuse. Glancing inside the car, I could see his eyes were closed and his head was hanging loosely. *He's too far over for me to reach him from the other door,* I realized.

My nose was assaulted by the smell of the gas just seconds before seeing the flames engulfing the tires. It quickly spread across the car, drinking up the liquid upon the windows. Continuing my assault on the window, my flesh began to blister from the heat before

I finally fell back against the rocks in exhaustion. *I can't get him out.*

My vision began to blur and my thoughts fell to my older brother, who was lying unconscious on the side of the hill, all alone. The last thing I heard before everything went black was a loud explosion.

Chapter

One

INDIGO
NINE YEARS LATER

Sweat trickled down my back, wetting my tank top, causing it to cling to my goose pimpled skin. The hair on my arm stood straight in the air, raised from an impending panic attack. This time it has woken me up. I know what brings them on. *Stress*. Though the fact that I seldom sleep through the night probably adds to it.

I remember the first time I had an attack. I was fifteen and I had awoken with a scream lodged in my throat. It took my parents almost an hour to calm me down. The attacks became a continual event, putting my parents perfect plan for me off track. Not every attack was the same, but they usually started with a sensation of the walls closing in around me, before I would break out in a cold, clammy sweat. My parents only tolerated it for so long before they eventually told me to let go of my dramatics. They brushed it off as an outcry for attention. It wasn't—but even if it were, they wouldn't have given me their attention. They were too busy arranging charity events, business meetings, and attending lavish dinners my brother and I were never allowed to attend. The obsessive drinking and the way they would sweep all of their obvious problems under a rug didn't help.

A year had passed before they finally gave into my psychosis, as mother would call it. An appointment was made with the best psychiatrist in New Hampshire that money could buy. Fortunately for me, Doctor Kinston lived up to her reputation. Much to my mother's dismay, she wouldn't discuss anything about our appointments. She would only say, "She's making progress, Jaquelyn, and that's all we can ask for. You should be proud." My mother didn't even know the meaning of proud. Cruel, cold-hearted wench—definitely, but proud wasn't in her vocabulary. She wasn't kind or loving. She was more of a Vodka-Tonic for breakfast, Whiskey by dinner kind of a person.

My father, on the other hand, was more of an, 'if it wears a skirt then it's getting attention' kind of a person. Neither one paid any attention to my brother or me. That's what the private schooling was for. We were rushed from practice, to events, to after school study programs, and evening gatherings, while at the same time being forced to hold an A average so we could attend the top colleges in the country. Not that it mattered, I'm sure if my parents made a large enough donation, I would have been able to get into any college I wanted.

I saw my family as a prison. The older I got, the tighter the bars pressed against my skin. When my mom started sleeping around with men in hopes to intentionally get caught by my father—well, that was the last straw. I refused to be a pawn in their games. I wouldn't choose a side, so they didn't choose me.

Instead they chose my brother to play back and forth, buying him expensive things and giving in to his every whim. It seems that apple didn't fall far from the tree. He's now on his second marriage and is currently drinking and cheating through that one as well.

That's what love is—lies, pain, and emptiness.

Sitting up, I pushed the sheets from my body before placing my bare feet against the cold wooden floors, and untwisting my dark gray pajama pants. The red numbers lit up on my alarm clock read three thirty-three. *The sun won't be up for a few more hours.*

Grabbing the hairbrush beside my clock, I combed it through my long black hair before pulling it back into a ponytail. Silently padding across the cold floor into the kitchen, I hit the button on my coffee maker and grabbed a mug from the cabinet. The blue light flickered on and I set my mug underneath it, allowing the fresh stream of coffee to fill it up. The smell alone helped to ease my nerves. Slipping my fingers around my cup of coffee, I place it to my lips. It was alarmingly hot, so I took slow, careful sips.

Every move I make is precise and calculated—part of my daily routine to help calm myself down. It's odd how something as simple as a dream can make you feel so on edge.

Walking toward the large glass windows framing the front of my New York City apartment, coffee in hand, I gently lowered myself to the floor. Crossing my legs in front of me, I leaned against the cold glass, watching as the city greeted the morning. Sighing, it suddenly hit me, *I finally feel at peace.*

My eyes followed the flow of traffic and I watched, mesmerized, as more people greeted the day, coming and going as they pleased. Occasionally I would take my fingers and make a pinching gesture against the glass. For just a moment, I felt like a giant taking out the civilians in the small town below me. *I should probably make an appointment to tell a therapist that—then again, I don't need anyone questioning my sanity.*

Rolling my shoulders, I glanced around my stark apartment. For being an interior decorator, my apartment is seriously deprived of flow and color schemes. Everything is gray or muted shades of whites and blacks. I've always had a knack for being able to see the

20

potential in almost any living space, but for some reason I just never applied it to my own space. It didn't help that most of it was now packed in boxes.

When I left New Hampshire at the young age of twenty-two, I opened my own interior decorating business out of the studio apartment I was renting at the time. In the last eight years I had turned my business from a dream into a reality. Indigo Designs was thriving. Between building my own company, avoiding my family, and leaving my cheating boyfriend, the stress had caused me to start having anxiety attacks again. The last one was so bad I didn't leave my apartment for two weeks. I desperately needed an escape.

Possession, or complete insanity, must have taken over me when I agreed to stay with my best friend from high school for the summer. Erin knew I had been stressed out lately, but I insisted it came with the territory of owning my own business. She insisted I needed to rebuild myself. *If she only knew just how right she is.*

As of yesterday, I'm no longer the owner of Indigo Designs. Everything here was closing in around me, so I decided to let it all go. Nick was my assistant for six years, so it only made sense for him to take over.

My flight leaves for Huntsville, Alabama, just after one o'clock this afternoon. Erin assured me my flight would go smoothly and she also promised me a chaos free vacation, but I still have my doubts. Either way, it was too late to change my mind, so by this time tomorrow I will be sleeping soundly in her guest bedroom.

My life used to be so organized. Everything fit perfectly into place and now all the pieces have shifted. Hopefully over the next few months I can pull myself back together.

Turning my head back toward the window, I pressed my face against the cold glass. Slowly sipping my coffee, I mentally went over every item I would need to take with me. I finished packing yesterday, but going over every detail eases my nerves and releases the tension from my impending panic attack.

At six o'clock I finally stood and made my way to the shower. *I might as well get ready to go. There's no sense in waiting until the last minute.*

From my seat I could hear a baby crying somewhere in front of me. I couldn't pinpoint their exact seat, but I'm certain whoever was near them is wishing for earplugs right now. The flight attendant passed by me in a flustered state, trying to pacify the heavier set man across the aisle from my row. He had been complaining of the noise from the children on the plane since we got off the ground. The arm of his seat appeared to be digging into his side, and I couldn't help but hope it felt as uncomfortable as it looked. The crying was getting on my nerves, but I had enough decency to keep my mouth shut. He on the other hand—I'm not so sure he was taught any manners whatsoever.

The elderly man next to me kept adjusting his glasses, as though the words in his book would become perfectly clear if he got them into the perfect position. He seemed sweet and smelled of vanilla, so I was thankful my window seat was next to him and not the rather angry, heavyset man across from us.

When the seatbelt sign came on everyone seemed to calm down a bit. I promised Erin I would call her as soon as I landed in Huntsville, but I think I'm going to wait until my feet have located a coffee shop. Caffeine is of utmost importance at this point in my travel.

The heavier set man made it off the plane before I did. However, in his hasty exit he failed to look down as his big galumphing feet tripped over the metal trim at the edge of the gate, causing him to fall flat on his big nose. *Karma. She's a beauty.* Two men in front of me helped him up, and made sure he was okay before continuing on their way. I just shook my head as I passed by. You get what you put out into this world. Be kind and it will be kind to you—at least that's the way it's supposed to work. It seems Karma is often out to get me, but I do love watching her take out others around me. We have a love/hate relationship—I love her and she hates me.

Making my way through the terminal, my nose smelled the coffee before I even saw it. Following the scent to a small kiosk just outside the gate, a younger guy, with long brown hair that was pulled back into a man bun, waited to take my order. His goatee was thinly spaced along his rather long chin, but I'm not entirely sure he was aware of how bad it looked. He flashed me a smile and a little wink as he handed me my drink. Rolling my eyes, I slung my purse over my shoulder. *Not today goatee boy, not today.* My standards may not be for everyone, but he doesn't even fit into my 'maybe' category. Make me laugh and you have a chance, but no amount of laughter would have helped him.

Taking a sip of my coffee, I was instantly filled with regret. *It's burnt.* Sighing, I take another sip. At this point I was desperate and I'd drink just about anything. As I reached my baggage claim, I pulled my phone out of my pocket to call Erin and let her know I had landed. The belt was circling the claim, but there were no bags yet. People were gathered around, waiting in metal seats and leaning against wide metal columns. I stood perfectly still, keeping my hands to myself. *God only knows what germs are spread across this place.* The woman behind me let out a rather loud cough, which only deepened my disgust.

My phone vibrated in my hand as all the notifications trickled in. Before I could even tap Erin's name on my screen, my phone began ringing. "Yes, dear?"

"Don't 'yes dear' me. Where are you? I'm assuming you've landed and didn't put everybody at risk by having your phone on."

"For your information, *mother*, I'm at baggage claim waiting for the airplane fairies to deliver my luggage to me via the dirty belt located in front of me. If you would like, I can snapchat you a picture of all of the germs."

"It's not that dirty. People clean it every day, Indie. Stop the dramatics. Are you sure you're okay with taking a cab? I can come get you, but it would be an hour or so."

"It will be fine. I'll be on my way once I grab my luggage, which seems to be lost in airplane fairyland because this belt has yet to produce it."

"Right. Well, the baby is crying and we both know Derek won't be able to handle her. I swear, if it's not in medical terms, he's useless. Lord knows he won't change a diaper."

"The bags are starting to arrive so I'm going to hop off anyway. Squish the baby for me and I'll see you in a bit."

Silencing my phone, I waited for my luggage to make its way around before grabbing it. Pulling up the handle I locked it into place and rolled it behind me as I headed toward the large glass doors opposite of me.

People were scattered everywhere, which could only be expected in an airport. Living in New York City, one would think I would be used to large amounts of people, but I'm still put off by mass hoards. At least when I was at home I had my set routine. The only time I ventured out was when I was working on a staging, and even then I was alone—aside from the furniture movers.

Looking down, I suddenly bumped into something. *Thank God, it's just a rope barricade and not a person. Plane. Coffee. Luggage. Cab.* I repeated the steps in my head and gathered my focus. A beautiful woman with perfect black braids twisted into a bun pulled up in a white cab. She gave me a bright white smile and I tossed my luggage in the backseat as I slid in. Using the sleeve of my sweater that was tied around my waist, I pulled the door shut.

It's not that I'm a germaphobe, I just prefer as little human contact as possible. I also prefer cleanliness and organization. I don't do well with dirt or clutter. Erin insists I don't mix well with people—under any condition. According to her, that's why I will never be able to hold down a solid relationship with anyone. Unfortunately, my ex-boyfriend, Kent, would most likely agree with her. He kept pushing things too far for my comfort. I wanted to take things slowly, and he wanted us to move in together. When I turned down the idea he took it as a green light to open our relationship up to other people. The problem was that he was the only one aware of this.

The sudden clearing of a throat brought my focus back to the woman driving the cab. Gathering my wits, I slipped her a sticky note with Erin's address written on it. She programed her GPS and we were on are way.

Erin's house is located off the beaten path—as she likes to call it. What she failed to mention was the immense size of her three-story brick home. Four huge white pillars ran up the front of her home, along with large white French style doors that stood out against the deep, rich color of the bricks.

Paying the driver for my fare, I grabbed my luggage and stepped out onto a stone-path driveway. *I wonder if this was laid by hand or if they used some sort of machine. Either way, I cannot fathom this being an inexpensive investment.* Suddenly, one of the large white doors flew open, and there stood my closest friend from high school just inside the doorway with her hair pulled back into a ponytail and the prettiest baby girl I have ever seen propped up on her hip. For the first time in a long time, I felt the yearning for a family tug at my soul. Sighing, I gave up on a life not meant for me, dropped my luggage and I ran up the porch steps and squeezed my friend tightly in my arms.

"God, I've missed you so much! Why did you have to move so far away?"

"I missed you too, babes. Hey, what's this? Indie, are you crying?"

Pulling away from our embrace I quickly wiped my cheeks while looking over my shoulder toward my suitcases, lying haphazardly in the drive. "What? No, I'm just tired."

"Come inside, I'll have Derek grab your things."

"Are you sure? I can do it. After all, I did put them in there, you know."

"It's not like he's busy. He's probably watching baseball in the office, while pretending to be working."

"Erin, really it's no big deal. If he's busy I don't want to bother him."

"He doesn't have a surgery scheduled for another week. He's not doing anything important. Come on in," she said, shifting the baby to her other hip as she kicked the door shut. "Derek? Can you grab Indie's things? She's exhausted." Her words fell sweetly from her lips as she gave me a wink.

The heels of my black boots clicked against the hardwood floors as I followed her into the kitchen. She moved with ease from one cabinet to another as she filled a snack cup and a bottle for the baby. Derek walked in from the adjacent door in the dining room and kissed the baby on the head before softly kissing the top of Erin's head. "Hey gorgeous, did I hear you call for me?"

"I did. Could you grab Indie's things? She's exhausted from the flight and the long drive. When you get done could you take Olivia for me for a bit?"

"Anything for you." he said, giving her a wink and lightly tapping her on the ass before grabbing my luggage, which was still standing by the front door. *I love the interactions between them.*

Since Erin went to college at Alabama University, I didn't have the pleasure of seeing her as often as I would have liked to. The first time I met Derek was when he was toasting my best friend at their rehearsal dinner. The next day was the wedding. Everything was so hectic that I never had the chance to fully introduce myself. I know he loves her, and he's given her an amazing life. For those reasons, I have added his name to the 'good guys' list. So far, besides my former assistant, Nick, he's the only one on it.

Plopping down on a barstool by the kitchen window, I propped my suddenly very tired, head up with my hand. "You guys are disgustingly adorable." I admitted.

"I know. He would do anything for me."

"It's gross." I crinkled up my nose for added effect.

"No it's not. This is how a relationship should be. Whatever you have with Kent is not a relationship." Carefully setting Olivia down on the floor with the snack cup, the baby's soft blonde ringlets fell around her face as she reached for the cereal with her chubby fingers. She must have noticed me watching because she looked up at me with the brightest blue eyes.

"Erin, she's absolutely gorgeous."

"She is." A soft smile graced Erin's features before she turned to me with an arched eyebrow. "Don't change the subject. We are talking about you and your lack of knowledge on relationships."

"I just got here. Couldn't we start with 'How is the weather in New York' first?' Why do you always feel the need to fix my love life?"

"You don't have a love life—you have a sex life. There's a difference."

"Says you. I'm quite content with it."

"And Kent?"

Brushing a few strands of loose hair behind my ear, I replied, "It's over. He cheated on me. I can't forgive him for that."

"You never told me that. When did that happen?" she asked in shock.

"It was right after the New Year. He wanted me to move in with him. I told him I couldn't, so he suggested he move in with me. I couldn't do that either. It's my space. Everything is just the way I like it, and I didn't want someone else to come in and mess it all up. You know? Apparently when I said no, I also said go sleep with your boss. I don't mind. Though, I don't remember saying the last bit."

Erin sat down in a chair across from me and reached for my hand. "I knew you had called it quits. I just wish you would've told me why." Her green eyes fell toward the baby now crawling around on the floor.

"It's not something I want to talk about." I admitted. Letting out a deep sigh I turned toward Derek as he walked in with my luggage rolling behind him. I've never been so thankful for a man in my life before. He must have created enough of a distraction for Erin that she forgot about being my relationship guru, because she started dictating to him where everything should go, as well as what Olivia was going to need. Ushering me to follow Derek, she mumbled to herself about fixing problems. *I hope I'm not one of them,* I thought to myself.

"I'm sure you're tired, I'll show you to your room and you can make yourself comfortable. How long will you be staying? I'm sure Erin's told me, but I can't seem to remember." Derek kindly asked.

"For the summer. I'm looking for my own place, I just don't know where."

Derek nodded his head as I walked behind him up the large oak stairs leading from the front door to the second floor. My fingers brushed along the intricately carved railing. I knew Erin's taste was very eclectic. She's always had a love for acquiring exquisite pieces from different time periods. As my eyes roamed the house I couldn't help but wonder how much of an influence she had in decorating, or if Derek had a say as well. The older pieces didn't clash with the modern ones, but instead they met in a way where one timeframe blended with the other. I couldn't have done a better job blending the two if I had tried.

Derek walked across the small landing at the top of the stairs before leading me up to the next floor. When we reached the top, he stopped at the first door he came to. My eyes were wide as I peered down the stairs behind us. *Erin has locked me away at the top of the tower like Rapunzel.* Derek, who must have read the confusion on my face, cleared his throat and offered me a sympathetic smile.

"Erin thought you might want a place to escape to. She knows how you enjoy your privacy. She said you would need a room with solitude."

"It's amazing how well she knows me. This is fine." The number of stairs I would have to climb is not something most people would look forward to, and to be honest, I wasn't looking forward to it either. *At least I will have my privacy, and my ability to lock away the world won't be compromised.* I smiled at Derek and took my luggage from him. I noticed a few thin lines on his forehead, along with two crinkles just on the outside of his eyes. *I bet his smile reaches his eyes,* I thought to myself. Erin was always attracted to tall blondes with blue eyes and a great smile. *It seems she finally caught one.*

"Let me know if you need anything else. The bathroom is just down the hall. There's not much up here, so it will just be you. There's an extra room just before the bathroom. That was Erin's office, but she doesn't use it anymore. Feel free to use it if you would like. I'm not sure what she has in there. It's mostly storage now."

"Thanks for letting me crash with you guys, Derek. I feel a lot more comfortable here than I would have in a hotel, where there are rampant amounts of bodily fluids sprayed everywhere."

He chuckled as he raised his eyebrows at my implications. "When Erin said you had a thing against germs, she wasn't kidding."

"I'm not sure if it's a germ thing, or more of a 'don't touch me because I don't know where you have been or what you have done thing.'" I admitted.

"Right. That's what we call a germ thing. I promise, everything in here is clean. The sheets and duvet are brand new so don't worry. No bodily fluids or germs are in the room. It's just you."

"Thank you."

"No problem. I have to get back downstairs and help with Olivia. Take your time getting settled."

"Thanks." I replied.

Stepping into room I rolled my suitcases into the corner beside the matching oak dresser with clawed feet. Upon first sight of the furniture I would have guessed them to be an early 1900's set, but as my fingers inspected the smoothness of the curves along the drawers I knew it was a modern piece. I softly pulled open a drawer and became pleasantly surprised by the red velvet lining. C.C. Grand Furniture Inc. was branded on the inside right corner of the drawer on a brass plate. Pulling my phone out of my pocket, I snapped a picture of the brass marking. *I might not have a place of my own yet, but eventually I will need some new furniture, and this would be perfect.*

Noticing the time on my phone, I plopped down on the large oversized bed. It was already after six. My stomach softly rumbled, but I ignored it. *I can eat later.* With utter exhaustion, I pulled a pillow under my head, closed my eyes and let the softness of the covers beneath me carry me off to sleep.

Chapter Two

The sound of someone calling my name pulled me from my slumber. My eyes slowly opened and I reluctantly sat up as Erin bounced on the end of the bed.

"Why are you sleeping? Seriously, you've done nothing but hide up here. Except your occasional cup of coffee or when you come down to eat. How much sleep could one person need?"

"I'm single with no responsibilities. Sleep is what I do."

Pulling at my arms, she dragged me from the heavenly pile of blankets and thrust me in front of the mirror. "This is what is happening. You're going to shower. Then you need to comb your hair or whatever is you feel you have to do to be ready to leave in one hour. I haven't had a drink in over a month and you are the perfect reason to celebrate."

Staring at the mirror, I realized just how far I'd let myself go. *This isn't like me. I need things to be neat and orderly, yet I'm gross and disheveled. Maybe a night out wouldn't be so bad.* "Fine, but only because I love you."

"Yes! That's my girl. This is going to be fantastic. Derek is driving, so we get a girl's night with a driver. We are going to bring down this town tonight," she said with excitement.

"I'm not sure how we are going to bring down a small town surrounded by farms and a golf course. Clubs aren't really my thing, babes. You know this."

"Indie, this is Alabama. We aren't going to a club—we're going to the pool hall. Throw some jeans on and meet me downstairs. You have one hour."

Erin bounced from the room and left me standing there wondering, *What happened to the girl from New Hampshire? We went to a private school where we were trained on social etiquette. We were graceful, perfected socialites, and now she's excited about a dirty pool hall? Time has changed her, or maybe she was this carefree before and I just didn't know it.*

My fingers brushed along the curve of the mirror as I compared our lives. For a split second, I was jealous of this new version of my friend, but I pushed it aside. *There's no reason to dwell on what she has that I don't.*

After a long, hot shower, I tossed my phone onto the bed after hitting play on my iTunes list. Andy Grammar's voice swirled around me as I rifled through my suitcases. I found a light blue, silk, tank halter-top with white lace along the collar that would look great with a pair of my dark skinny jeans. Pulling on the shirt, I grabbed a clip from my makeup bag before pulling my hair up into a messy knot on the top of my head. Running my fingers through a few loose strands, I twisted them into little waves. Pinching my cheeks for some added color, I brushed on a few coats of mascara, and threw some red lipstick on for good measure.

Slipping into my jeans I glanced over my image in the mirror. A beautiful woman stared back at me. *She looks so put together, but looks can be deceiving.* Slipping my feet into my black flats, I grabbed my clutch from the top of the dresser and headed down the stairs. I could hear Erin moving about in the kitchen, dictating to some poor soul I'm sure she has cornered. Just as I walked around the corner, Derek stepped out of the kitchen shaking his head.

"For your sake, I wouldn't go in there. She's lecturing Clarissa on how to properly rinse and sanitize the bottles. The poor girl has to endure this every time we go out."

"Do you guys go out often?" I asked out of curiosity.

"No. It's hard to get a sitter—and now you know why."

Laughing, I walked into the kitchen. *Derek may not know how to pull her away, but I do. Besides, someone had to rescue the poor girl Erin had locked in there with her.*

"Erin, are we leaving or not? You woke me up and made me shower when pajama pants and Netflix were the better option. I turned down bingeing on a new series and indulging in the chocolate I smuggled into my suitcase to go out with you. Get your crap and let's go."

Clarissa turned her head toward me with a shocked look in her eyes. *Maybe I am the only person who knows how to rein Erin in.*

"Indie, Olivia could hear you."

"Well, *mother*, I guess we should go then. I wouldn't want to poison the princess with my eccentric vocabulary. Besides, you and I both know you wouldn't leave her with just anyone. You obviously chose this Clarissa person for a reason. Let her do her job so we can go. It's why you pay her." I smiled softly at the sitter before raising my eyebrows toward Erin. I was daring her to challenge me and she knew it.

"Fine. We can go. It's just that I get worried."

Linking my arm through hers I led us out of the kitchen, leaving Clarissa to tend to the sweet baby in the highchair. "It's okay to worry—I get it. But this is a friendly reminder, I am here to relax. If I wanted to spend time with a pretentious, controlling mother I would have gone to New Hampshire to see my own mother. I wouldn't have flown four hours to be with my best friend."

"That's true. How is Jaquelyn doing anyway?"

"I wouldn't know. The last I heard she had a new boy toy and my dad was in search of yet another piece of arm candy. It's disgusting how they stay married to one another."

Nodding her head, she stepped through the front door. Derek followed behind us, his eyes wide in utter disbelief as we walked toward their black sedan. He stepped around me and helped me into the backseat, while Erin climbed into the front passenger side.

Shocked, he asked, "How did you get her to do that?"

"It took years for me to master the skill of distracting her. Don't worry—it won't last long. Soon she will be focused on lecturing some other poor soul and I have a feeling it's going to be me." Derek laughed and closed my door before hopping into the driver's seat.

It wasn't long before we were lost along the scattered lights of the highway. Small clusters of lights clung together before breaking away into the darkness of night again. My eyes tried to catch the stars in the night sky, but there were too many clouds covering the view. I felt let down in a way. *I was promised stars and beauty beyond measure, but instead, my view consists of the inside of a car and wispy clouds.*

Pulling up in front of a red brick building, we stepped out of the car and my eyes took in my surroundings. Across the peak of the entryway, the name *Hollows* in neon blue lit up the dark night. The red front door opened letting light and loud music trickle out as two people, twisted together, stumbled into the parking lot. Derek helped Erin step out as I walked around the car toward the light, like a moth to the flame. Normally I'm cautious of a new place, situations, and people, but this time I had no reservations. It was a new feeling for me—but I was totally going with it.

We walked in and I immediately noticed my ballet flats were sticking to the dark cement floor. Dark wood paneling and trim surrounded the rooms, and I could hear the balls clicking against one another on the billiard tables in the corner. Derek found a tall table tucked against the wall, near an open space between tables currently being used as a dance floor. Surprisingly, this bar was different than what I expected. I was expecting southern clichés, like people line dancing and mechanical bulls but it was just a small, hometown bar.

Erin and I made ourselves comfortable as Derek left to get us some drinks. Brushing invisible dirt off my jeans, I looked around, finding several eyes on me. "Do I stand out that bad?" I asked.

Erin smiled as she took her drink from Derek. "No, sweetie. I think most people here know each other, that's all. You're new. The looks will stop, I promise. Even I was stared at, at one time."

Nodding my head, I rolled my shoulders and shook off the unease starting to crawl over my skin. We fell into conversation as though we hadn't had miles separating our lives from one another. *I haven't felt this relaxed in a long time.*

"Look, I'll give you tonight—but tomorrow we are working on you. You haven't told me anything besides you and Kent not being an item anymore. I need details, Indie. I miss being front and center for the drama that is your life."

"You're one to talk. What happened to the bridezilla who threw a fit at her wedding over the napkins being the wrong shade of peach? Which, for the record, I still don't think was a friendly color for any of the girls to be wearing."

"It wasn't about you, though. I wanted to look good. If I needed to dress you down to do it, then so be it. I'll have you know, Derek paid a lot for those napkins. They were supposed to be silk, not whatever polyester concoction they laid on the tables. The color was completely off. Everyone noticed."

Sipping my drink, I shook my head. "No, babe—*you* noticed. No one else cared because they were too focused on the fact that your bridesmaids were the color of vaginas."

Erin's eyes went wide as Derek spit his beer across the table. *I forget how crass I can sometimes be. I guess he's not used to it yet.* She gently pat him on the back while he tried to compose himself.

"Wow—sorry about that. I can honestly say that's the first time I've ever heard anyone say that. On that note, I'm going to go get a refill." Laughing, Derek headed over to the bar. Watching him walk away, Erin swiped her tongue over her bottom lip as she checked him out. *She still thinks her husband is attractive. I find it to be an adorable quality.*

"You know if you were, well if you weren't so…I don't know—you, you could have a nice husband like that too. Maybe even a family."

"Nope, stop right now. This conversation is not happening. I love my life and I'm not in a place to add the drama of a husband or family. That would be messy and would interfere with my plans."

"And what are your plans? Dying of old age? You're going to end up alone with no one to comfort you, other than your thirteen cats. And do you know what's going to happen? They are going to eat you after you die because there will be no one there to tell them not to."

"What kind of morbid hell do you picture me living in? Cats eating corpses? Sweetie, there's something definitely wrong with you. I'm getting a drink and possibly something to eat." Grabbing my clutch off the table I headed to the bar for a drink, maybe even a shot. *I love her, but she can really press my buttons.*

Derek was leaning against the edge of the bar, patiently waiting for the bartender to turn around. I smiled as I took a seat on the black leather barstool beside him. Titling his head to side he gave me a slight smirk. "What did she say?"

"Nothing. She just thinks she knows what's best for me. How did you know she said something?"

"Don't get me wrong, she's my wife and I love her, but she often chews her own feet."

"That's an interesting way to describe it."

Catching the beer the bartender slid across the table, Derek leaned over my shoulder. "You coming back to the table or can I snag my wife for a dance?"

"Snag away. I'm a big girl. What's the worst that could happen? I get hit on by some cowboy wearing plaid?"

"Just be careful. That's easily done around here." Nodding his head around the room, he headed back over to where Erin was sitting. My eyes took in the crowd and I suddenly noticed the plaid shirts and blue jeans heavily speckled throughout the mass of people gathered in groups around the tables and billiards.

"What can I get ya?" A gruff voice yelled over the loud music pouring from the speakers on the corner of the bar.

"Excuse me?" Looking up I saw the bartender toss a towel over his shoulder.

"What's your poison? What do you want to drink?" the bartender asked.

"Oh, sorry. Um, can I have a shot of Jack and a Whiskey Sour?"

"Sure thing." He spun around, grabbing a shot glass from the glass shelves behind him. My fingers tapped idly against my clutch as I waited for my drinks. I was doing my best to avoid touching the bar. If the floor was any indication of cleanliness, I wasn't taking my chances with the bar.

"You must have confused him." Turning my head, my eyes fell on an overly confident man leaning his back against the bar.

"And how have I done that?"

"Well, normally, Tim is quick with drinks, but you got him huffing and puffing back there." Spinning his chair around, he rested his forearms on the edge of the bar. My eyes roamed across the span of his broad shoulders. He's bigger than me, but it didn't put me off. Instead, I became cockier.

Rolling my eyes, I spied the heavyset bartender coming back with my drinks. "It's just a drink. Don't worry yourself over it, I wouldn't want you to hurt yourself."

"Huh, so it is. Maybe it's you he's so worked up about. I don't blame him though."

"Oh my God, if this is your version of a pickup line, please stop right now."

"Ha! That would make for an awful one. Don't ya think? I can do better than that."

Grasping the shot glass in my hand I slammed the liquor back and reveled in the burn before chasing it with two large sips from my cocktail. I raised my brow to the man beside me. "Look, I get it, I'm the new girl in the bar. I'm like a bright, shiny new toy that all the boys want to play with. I'm not here to meet anyone, I just want to relax and enjoy my drink without strangers hitting on me."

"Well aren't you full of yourself? Who said I was hitting on you anyway? I do believe you sat down next to me, all smug in your cute little top. Why would I spend my time hitting on someone so pretentious?"

"Pretentious?" I asked.

"I know. This is hard for you to take in, isn't it? I mean with me being so incredibly good looking and educated. Who knew us cowboys in plaid would have such charm?"

Closing my eyes, his words fell over me. *He must have overheard me talking to Derek. It seems Erin isn't the only one putting her foot in her mouth tonight.*

"I have nothing against plaid...or cowboys. That's not what I meant by that."

"No? Then why so cold?"

"I don't do this. I'm not one to let a guy pick me up at a bar, let alone a stranger."

"Who say's I'm trying to pick you up? You just keep assuming I'm interested. You haven't even told me your name yet. What if it's a hideous name? What if it completely turns me off?"

He's baiting me. I knew it, but I still took the bait. Sighing, I turned to face him. "You're not getting my name and I don't want yours either."

"Hmm…yet you don't want to talk to a stranger either. You do realize you and I are having a conversation?" He smirked and I noticed small creases by the corners of his eyes. I couldn't quite make out their color because the lighting was absolute shit. *Perhaps they are a light brown like the hair tousled in a mess on the top of his head.* He must have caught me staring because he slowly ran his hand through it, fixing the wayward strands of hair. "Maybe you're the one hitting on *me.*"

Heat rose to my cheeks from my embarrassment at being caught. "What? I am not! Besides, I don't talk to strangers and this is not a conversation. This is me—rejecting you."

"Fine. Have it your way." Turning, he grabbed his beer from the bar and walked away. *I have no idea what it is about him, but the way he talks doesn't just get on my nerves, it gets under my skin. Why do all the good-looking ones have to be assholes?* Shaking the random thoughts from my already too crowded mind, I slammed the rest of my drink and set the glass on the counter, motioning to the bartender for another one.

"Can I get some chips or something to soak up the liquor, please?" The bartender nodded his head as he made me another drink.

"Chips and a drink." the bartender said, placing my order in front of me.

I laughed as the bartender handed me a bag of barbecued potato chips along with my drink. I slapped two twenties on the counter. "No change. What I don't spend you can keep." I don't wait for a response. Instead, I dive into my bag of overly greasy potato chips. It wasn't my first choice for a snack, but the options here were pretty limited.

"Excuse me, Miss, do you mind if I sit here?" A rather polite voice caught my attention. Brushing my hands off on a small bar napkin, I looked up. My blood began to boil as I realized the stranger was back. *He is not giving up easily.*

Irritated, I asked, "What do you want now?"

"Hi there, Miss. I just wanted to say hello." He extended his hand and against the better part of my judgment I placed my hand in his. "The name's, *Not a Stranger.* It's nice to meet you."

My head tilted back as laughter fell from my lips. *He's playful––and cute. I guess it can't hurt to make a friend.* I give in with a shake of my head. "Well done. I have to say, I'm slightly impressed."

"Really? I had some good pickup lines I was certain would catch your attention."

"Now I'm disappointed. Though, I can't imagine what you could have said, that I haven't already heard. Being hit on in bars in New York is like being rained on in Seattle. It's unavoidable."

Laughing, he nodded to the bartender who slid him another beer. The light hit his eyes and I realized they weren't brown like I originally thought. Instead, they were a deep blue. "Disappointed huh? I don't like the sound of that. Maybe you can help me pick out a few good lines I can use to pick up some other woman, since you're clearly not interested in anything other than those chips." he said, nodding toward the bag of chips in front of me.

"I have a healthy appetite. It's not a bad thing." I squinted my eyes, wondering to myself what he could be up to. Deciding to play along with *Mr. Not a Stranger*, I flashed him a challenging smile. "Alright, let's hear them."

Clearing his throat, he spun his barstool to face me. "Hey, baby, feel this shirt. You know what kind of material this is? It's boyfriend material."

"Oh, that's just awful. That has to be one of the lamest one's I've ever heard."

"You can do better?"

"Of course I can. Are you a baker? Cause you have some hot buns."

Laughing, he took a sip of his beer. "You just made that one up."

"I did not. Some guy tried to hit on me over the New Year with that one."

"Well he did a horrible job. I got a better one. Are you Google? Because I've just found what I'm looking for."

Sipping my drink, I shook my head. "No—just no. Those are way too polite. You need to get sleazier with them."

"Sleazier huh? Any suggestions?"

"Okay, how about this one? It's a good thing I have my library card on me...because I'm totally checking you out."

"What? That's not sleazy. If we are going to do this, we need to do this right." He raised his hand motioning for the bartender. "Tim, we are going to need a bottle of Jack and some shot glasses over here. Put it on my tab."

"Oh no, I'm not having anyone buy me drinks. I can buy my own."

With an arch of his brow and a dangerous smirk on his face, Mr. Not a Stranger turned back to the bartender. "Fine then, put it on her tab. I'm okay with that."

My mouth fell open at his suggestion. "I am not paying for all of your drinks either."

"Then it's settled—Tim, put it on my tab."

Smug bastard. He knows exactly what he is doing. Tim laughed as he set two shot glasses and a full bottle of amber colored liquor in front of us. Mr. Not a Stranger unscrewed the cap and filled the glasses to the top. "So, this is how this will work. We are each going to give each other a pick-up line. If you can't keep a straight face, you take a shot."

Feeling rather confident in my ability of turning down pickup lines I nodded in agreement. "I'll go first. I lost my number, can I have yours?"

"That's a good one, but no one is going to fall for that. Besides, the goal is sleazy."

"Fine. You do better."

"Is that a mirror in your back pocket? Cause I can definitely see myself in your pants."

A giggle escapes my lips before I remembered our bargain. I slammed back my shot and watched as he filled it back to the top. *My throat burns, but I'm not losing this game.* "Hi, I'm Indie. Remember that—because you'll be screaming it later."

"Indie? That's unique. I like it." he said with a smile.

I mentally kick myself for giving away my name. "Okay, forget that one. I have a better one anyway. If I told you that you have a beautiful body would you hold it against me?"

"Lame. That was so lame. Come on, we have to do better than that. How about you sit in my lap and we'll talk about the first thing that pops up?" He laughed before he could even get the last word out. "I'm sorry, even I know that was awful." He slammed back a shot, poured himself another one and slammed it back as well.

"Two shots?" I questioned. "I didn't think it was that funny."

"Oh, no——the second shot is for the next one. Don't judge me too harshly, okay?"

"It's too late. I've been judging you since I sat down. I can't just stop because you've asked me to, so this better be good."

He held up his hand trying to compose himself. "I'm going to call you Skittles, cause baby, I want to taste the rainbow."

Applauding his win, I laughed while taking another shot. "That one took me by surprise."

"I'm glad. Since we now have an official conversation going, may I ask what brought you here?"

"It's not a what—it's a who. She's over there dancing with her husband." His eyes followed my finger pointed in the direction of Erin. His brow furrowed as he turned back to face the bar. "What's the matter? Do you know Erin?"

"No. I can't say that I've had the pleasure of meeting her. I know Derek, though. He's a good guy."

A slender figure walked in, catching his attention. Suddenly, his back straightened and he quickly stared forward, as though I wasn't still sitting on my barstool. And just like that the playful banter between us died. My eyes flashed across the room to where Erin was walking back to the table. I waited for my stranger to say something, but instead he was quiet as he nursed the beer in front of him. *I guess whatever fun we were having is over.*

Grasping my clutch in my hand, I carefully hopped down from the barstool. "Look, I'm not used to enjoying other people's company—I just thought you should know I enjoyed yours. Take it however you want." He didn't turn around, he just sat completely silent, nursing his drink. Knowing when I'm not welcome, I headed back to the table where Erin and Derek were holding hands and giggling over what I can only assume are private secrets.

"So, who was that?" Erin asked.

"Who was what?"

"Don't avoid my question with a question, Indie. I invented that trick—just ask Derek. I do it every time I go shopping." Erin sipped on her beer while Derek tried his best to hide his smirk.

"She ain't lying either. That's exactly what she does. Anytime I open one of my credit card bills she has a million questions."

Kicking him under the table, she placed her hand defiantly on her hip. "And it works, so let it be. Indie, ignore Derek, all I'm saying is I haven't seen you smile in a long time. You were having fun. Admit it."

Sighing, I slipped my arms from my rather warm jacket and hung it on the back of the chair. "Okay, fine—it was fun, but I don't know his name. If you want any other information, you'll have to ask him yourself."

"You didn't get his name? That whole time you were flirting and you didn't even ask his name." Erin shook her head, "If you didn't exchange names, what did you talk about the entire time you were over there?"

Smiling to myself, I placed my clutch on the table. "Plaid shirts and skittles." A small laugh escaped me causing Erin to roll her eyes at my response.

"Darling, I know you want Indie to make friends, but maybe it's best to let this one be. He's not a fan of attention. In fact, I'm quite surprised he talked to her to begin with. Perhaps it's just best if we let whatever happened be."

Chewing on my thumbnail, I glanced over my shoulder to look for my *Not a Stranger*, but I didn't see him anymore. *What a shame,*

I kind of liked him. My attention was drawn back to the table at the sound of Erin's voice steadily climbing to higher notes.

"Derek, who was he? And you can't tell me you don't know...I already asked you and you said you didn't know. Oh. My. God. You lied to me!" *Now this is the Erin I know.* She has always been the first to inhale new rumors and secrets while being incredibly over dramatic. I always thought she would have done well on a daytime soap opera.

"Calm down—I didn't lie to you. I used to know him. We used to play ball together, but that was a long time ago. I don't know who he is anymore." Derek's voice took a steady, firm tone. I never pictured him as being the authoritative type, but by the way he was trying to put his foot down, I was clearly mistaken.

Erin and I looked at one another in complete shock. I was about to list off a thousand questions when she leaned over, almost falling out of her chair. "Fine, I won't say another word." In her drunken state, she attempted to lock her lips with an invisible key, but ended up locking her cheek instead.

Derek cleared his throat and changed the conversation to the prospects of Alabama's football team. *It's April and he's already discussing the sport as if it's happening right now.* Erin hung on to his every word. I, on the other hand, got completely lost in my thoughts.

Scanning the room again, my eyes checked every plaid shirt to see if it was my mystery guy. I was just about to give up hope when I noticed him stepping out of the hallway near the bar. The urge to talk to him again was getting hard to ignore.

Despite my better judgment, I headed toward him, pretending as though I was headed to the restroom. I could see him turning toward the bar when I lowered my head and purposely bumped into his arm.

"Most people look up when they walk." he stated.

"Sorry, it was an accident." Looking up, I saw him staring back at me with his head tilted to the side. *I'm caught.*

"Was it? Because I'm almost certain I spotted you across the room just a few seconds ago. You must have moved pretty fast to end up over here bumping into me. Not to mention how stealthy you must be to not bump into anyone else while looking at the ground."

Well shit. What do I say to that? My idea of asking him where the bathroom was has gone completely out the window. Now he's standing here in front of me, calling me out on my bullshit. Sighing, I waved the white flag and admitted my defeat. "Fine, you caught me. It was intentional, okay. Are you happy now?" I asked in defeat.

"That depends, are you coming over here because Derek said something or because you want to be?"

"Yes, to both. He was rather vague though. He wouldn't say anything other than you two used to play ball together. My friend even tried to coerce him to reveal your name, and he stuck to your secrecy, causing him to lie to his wife and mother of his only child. It's sad really. One lie can cause such a rift."

Chuckling he ran his fingers through his hair. "You bumped into me on purpose, now you are trying to guilt-trip me into telling you secrets—I'm not revealing anything. Not until you tell me the other reason why you bumped into me."

"This may come as a shock to you, but I'm not a people person. In fact, I hate dealing with people in general. I used to, but I don't have to anymore. Now, it's just me." Realizing I was rambling, I clamped my lips shut.

"I have no clue what you are talking about. You've completely lost me."

"Sorry, I do that. It's part of my charm. Like I said before, I don't like people."

Confused, he asked, "Why is that important to me?"

Why is this so difficult? "Because I liked you, or at least I thought I did—or do. I don't know. This is weird. I'm going back to my table now." *Why did I think this was a good idea?*

I started to take a step away from him when my shoe suddenly had other ideas. My foot lifted from the floor, but my ballet flat was stuck. The sticky cement floor had officially claimed ownership of it. Not wanting to put my foot on the floor, I tried my best to balance myself while bending over to grab my shoe. Unfortunately, balancing has never been my forte. I started to tumble forward, so I squinted my eyes shut and braced my arms in front of me, anticipating the sticky floor claiming the rest of me as well.

Grabbing ahold of my shoulders, my stranger asked, "Whoa—how many drinks have you had?"

His voice caused me to jolt as my hands wrapped around the wrists gripping my shoulders. Our eyes met, and my voice completely abandoned me. Not one sound or a word of thanks fell from my lips. Helping me to stand, he pulled my shoe from the floor. In one swift move he lifted me from the floor and set me on a barstool before sliding my lost shoe onto my foot. Thoughts of Cinderella filled my head, but I dismissed them to being fairy tales. *I don't want or need a prince to save me—or my shoes.*

"Are you okay, or do you need a minute?"

"I'm not drunk. It's the damn floor—it's so sticky. It stole my shoe." I whined.

"Don't blame the floor for you wearing ballerina slippers to a bar."

"How was I supposed to know the floor would be gooey?" I swallowed, focusing on his words instead of his close proximity to me, which was making me second-guess everything.

Running his hands through his hair, his blue eyes looked down at me. "It's just that most people wear normal shoes."

"Flats are normal." I stated flatly. My mood flashed from flirty to irritation within a matter of seconds with him. *There's just something about him.*

"In the city, maybe, but here? You need some boots—or at least some shoes that can handle sticky situations. Though it doesn't matter now. You've already admitted you like me, and now I've saved you from a horrible, sticky floor, so you have to repay the favor." The corner of his lip curled up. *He's smirking at me and somehow I find him just as irritating as I find him attractive.*

Pressing my lips together tightly, I inhaled through my nose before releasing a sigh as I relented to the situation. "And how does one repay a favor of such magnitude?"

"That's easy—you dance with me." He held his hand out and I reluctantly slipped mine into his, as my mystery man led us to the dance floor. Sliding one hand around my waist, he pulled me towards him as he grasped my hand and placed it on his shoulder. His feet slowly moved side to side. *This dance is all wrong. The music is fast and loud, and he's moving us to a much slower tempo. It's as though he's hearing a completely different song.*

"Why are we dancing like this?"

"Why not? I don't like this song. It's too fast for us. This is my rhythm when I dance with you. You don't like it?"

A smile played on my lips as I looked up at this strange man I'd found myself with. "I like it." I felt so light on my feet with him. It was as though I was actually floating.

"Good." He spun me away from him and slowly brought me back with a pull of his fingers. The smell of his cologne surrounded me. As we danced the stress from the last year fell away, and for the first time in a long time, I felt comfortable in my own skin. I felt beautiful.

We danced that way for two more songs, until we were interrupted by Derek. "Indie, I'm sorry to say this, but I think she's tapped out of fun for the night." He nodded his head to where Erin was, barely sitting up in her chair. She was hunched over, leaning against the table.

My eyes glanced from Derek to my mystery man and back to Derek again. *As much as I want to see where this could go, I need to make sure my friend is okay.* "Yeah, I guess. I mean—if she's done, then so am I. Let's get her home."

"Wait." There was a slight sadness in my dance partner's eyes as he gripped my hand, stopping me from walking away. "I forgot to mention it's my birthday. This—you—it's the best present I've had in a while. Thank you. I just wish there was some way I could convince you to stay with me."

"I'm sorry, but I don't know you yet. Happy Birthday though." Reaching up on my toes I softly placed a kiss on his cheek. I stepped out of his arms and helped Derek walk Erin to the car. *Never in my life have I felt more disappointed in timing than I do right now. A few more songs and I would have been putty in his hands.* The thought of his hands on me leaves me wanting something I told myself I wouldn't do. *No hookups. I don't need to jump from one mess to another.* I mentally chastised myself.

The front door clatters against the wall behind us as I opened my car door. "Wait!" Turning around, I saw my stranger yelling at me just outside the entrance to the bar.

"She needs to go." I said, pointing towards Erin, as he jogged over toward me.

"I know, but I needed to tell you something."

"What?" My eyes flashed towards Derek, who was sliding into the driver's seat after buckling Erin's seat belt.

"I lied." Leaning his hand against the frame of the car he slowly leaned over me. "It's not my birthday. I just wanted you to stay."

"Oh."

"But if it were my birthday I would want to spend it with you."

Laughing, I asked, "More pickup lines? I thought we were past that."

Running his hands through his hair his tongue softly brushed his lower lip. "I can do better than that."

Waiting for another pick up line, I was taken by surprise when his hand wrapped around my neck, grasping my face, while bringing his lips to mine. Heat scorched my body and little electric shocks stung my lips as I twisted my hands in his hair. The feeling of floating came back, and I drifted away as he slowly broke our kiss. His eyes met mine, and I knew whatever it was that I had felt, he felt it too. I'm not a believer in instant love connections. No one falls in love the first day they meet, but I couldn't deny the current I felt between us. Attraction? Lust? I'm not sure what it was, but I wanted to feel it again.

"Indie, we have to go." Derek cut in.

Nodding my head, I looked back over at Derek, who was becoming impatient with me. I don't blame him, my friend needs me and I'm kissing random guys in a parking lot. "Sorry, Derek."

"Sorry, this one's on me. I couldn't just let her leave." Derek nodded his head as my stranger closed my door. I clicked my seatbelt into place and laid my head against the cool window as my fingers traced the plump curves of my lips that were still stinging from our kiss.

As we pulled out of the parking lot, I turned back to look for my stranger. He was standing underneath the lights by the entrance as a slender shadow approached him. I watched curiously as the shadow waved its arms about before walking back inside, leaving him all alone in the dark.

Ignoring the jealousy creeping into my mind, I brushed my lips again with my fingers. *My first night out went so much better than I expected. I wonder what tomorrow will bring.*

Chapter

Three

Coffee. It is the first thing my senses pick up on. For the first time in a long time, I slept through the night. I don't know if it's this insanely comfortable bed, the fresh air, or the handsome stranger I've dreamt about for the last week. Whatever it was, I hope it works again. Pushing the covers off of me, I slipped my feet into my slippers while pulling my hair into a messy knot. Normally I wouldn't be caught dead looking like this—but coffee—I need it.

I could hear sweet giggles coming from the living room as I descended the stairs from my tower. *I have no idea how Erin gets up so early each morning and remains chipper throughout the day. It must be witchcraft.* As I continued my descent, the voices in the house grew louder. When I reached the living room, Erin was playing on the floor with Olivia, who was chewing on what looked like a rubber giraffe.

"Indie, you've been asleep forever. I wanted to go up there and wake you, but Derek insisted I leave you alone."

My eyes glanced over to Derek, who was sitting in a leather recliner, sipping on his coffee while reading a newspaper. He gave me a soft smile and went right back to reading. *I can't even remember the last time I touched a printed newspaper. All of my subscriptions are electronic.*

When I was little, my dad would hide under a pile of newspapers every morning. I remember how he would smell of ink when I would wrap my arms around him to say goodbye before school. It's such an odd memory to hold on to, but then again, it's one of the few I like.

"So, what are the plans for today? I hope it revolves around coffee and naps."

"I can't tell if you're being serious or sarcastic right now."

"Let's just go with both."

"And here I thought if you got more sleep, you would be less of a brat."

Laughing, I walked into the kitchen and headed toward the counter before pouring myself the fresh cup of coffee my body so desperately needed. "And that's where you went wrong. I'm always a brat."

"I'm not sure how I could have forgotten that." Erin yelled from the living room. I giggled to myself while taking a sip of the heaven in my mug.

"I'm taking my coffee back upstairs. Then I'm going to shower. Can you please tell me what we are doing so I know what to wear?" Taking two huge gulps of the hot, heavenly liquid, I peered over my mug. Erin was still lying on the floor while Olivia crawled all over her. *Motherhood suits her perfectly.*

"I was planning a day at the spa, but Logan called and he wants me to come look at the sketches for the rocking chairs he's designing for the children's auction at the hospital next month, so I'm taking you with. You'll love it."

"Am I supposed to know who Logan is?"

"No, but he owns CC Grand. He's the one who designed the furniture in your room."

This will give me a better opportunity to see some more of their work. I thought to myself. "Give me thirty minutes and I'll be ready."

After taking a record-breaking shower, I twisted my hair up into a bun before digging through my clothes. I settled for a pair of jean shorts and a black t-shirt with a picture of the band Queen on the back of it. Bohemian Rhapsody was written in faded white letters on the front. Grabbing a black ribbon from my makeup bag, I tied it into a bow around my throat before slipping my feet into a pair of slip-on black sandals. Tossing my phone into my clutch, I headed downstairs.

Erin had the baby on her hip and a diaper bag slung over her shoulder. "You ready? Derek had an emergency at the hospital so Olivia is coming with us."

Nodding, I followed her to their sedan. I watched as she carefully placed the baby in the car seat, double-checking to make sure she was buckled in properly. Sliding into the driver's seat, she gave me a big grin before turning the key. "I think we have everything. Let's get this show on the road."

Erin pushed a few buttons on her steering wheel and soon Mozart was coming through the speakers. Raising my eyebrow, I silently questioned her choice in music, but I didn't say a word. Matching me eyebrow for eyebrow she threw the car into reverse. "Don't judge me. Classical music is known for helping children learn."

"Not judging, just wondering who you are and where my crazy friend from high school has gone. You know, the one that was arrested for streaking across the tennis courts?"

"I'll have you know, I wasn't arrested. It was a simple misunderstanding. Once they talked to my dad they let me go."

"Because he paid them." I stated matter of fact.

"He did not. He made a little donation."

"Right—he paid them."

"Whatever. It doesn't matter now. That was a long time ago. I have Olivia now, and I want to make sure she gets the best of everything."

Olivia let out a squeal of excitement as we turned onto the road. Looking at her in the rear-view mirror, I returned her smile. "I'm excited too, kid."

I hope this place is what I am looking for.

Gravel crunched underneath the tires as we drove up the road. *What is with this place and why are there so many gravel roads? Surely someone has heard of asphalt. They definitely need more of it.*

As we pulled up to the old, white farmhouse with gray shutters and a rather large covered porch, two red pole barns set back just off to the side of the house came into view. CC Grand was written in black letters above the smaller barn's large, white doors.

Erin parked the car and grabbed Olivia from the backseat. I stepped out and took the diaper bag from Erin, trying to help lessen her load. As we walked toward the white doors, I noticed a cement ramp with black railing on the side of the house. A paved path led from the ramp to the side of the barn, looking very out of place against the gravel.

As we stepped into the barn, we were immediately assaulted with the smell of cedar and varnish. The front of the barn had a small office with a glass window looking out into the warehouse. Lumber was piled up against the walls and several pieces of furniture were scattered about in the center. Each piece was in a different phase of completion. A chair with intricately carved arms and matching lion's feet caught my attention. The dark walnut stain accentuated the deep curves in the wood.

"Is it the chair or the mirror that has caught your attention?" A deep baritone voice pulled my gaze from the window. Turning, I found a very handsome man seated at the desk in the corner, looking over blueprints. His dark hair was short and neatly parted to one side with bright blue eyes blinking up at me. *There's something about him—almost as if I have seen him before, but that's impossible.* Clearing his throat, he arched a brow.

Attempting to act as though I wasn't staring, I turned back to the window. "The chair. Did you make all of these?" I asked.

"No, I designed them. Someone else builds them. Forgive me if I don't get up to greet you, but Mrs. Whitt and I need to see to these plans." His deep voice was firm and cold. I wondered for a split second what could have made him so sharp with his words, but then again, perhaps I was just looking for a problem that wasn't there.

"Oh—no, you're fine. I think I'll look for that mirror now."

Erin sat down at the desk with Olivia in her lap and they began discussing textures and colors while I stood by the window, gazing into the warehouse in search of a mirror. A tarp covering a rather oblong shape was leaning against one of the walls. It was the only piece that resembled the shape of a mirror, but I found it odd that they would cover it, and not any of the other pieces.

I'm not sure how long we had been cooped up in that small office, but it was long enough for Olivia to become fussy. *It seems sitting still isn't her forte.* Erin gave me a pleading look, so I walked over and took the baby from her arms. Adjusting the diaper bag strap on my shoulder, I stepped outside into the bright sun.

"We will be outside should you need us."

Seeing a tall tree surrounded by a patch of grass next to the other barn, we slowly made our way toward it. I walked along the edge of the building, keeping Olivia shaded in its shadow until my feet hit the grass. Shrugging the diaper bag off my shoulder, I dropped it to the ground before setting Olivia down on the plush ground. She picked at a couple blades before crawling over to the tree. I followed her and watched in awe as she inspected every detail around her.

A sudden loud crash, followed by some very loud yelling caused me to jump. Pressing my hand to my chest I peered in the direction of the barn. *Whoever—or whatever is in there is not having a good time.* My eyes grew wide and I quickly snatched Olivia from the grass as a hammer landed a few feet away from us. My heart was slamming in my chest. *What the hell was that?* A shadow appeared from the side door of the barn and I let loose.

"What the fuck is wrong with you? You could have fucking killed her? Jesus Christ! You're an adult—fucking act like one. Stomping around and throwing tools must be the most idiotic way of dealing with a problem. I swear to God, if I wasn't holding her I would be kicking your ass."

"What the hell?" A deep familiar voice catches me off guard.

The shadow stepped out into the sun and my jaw dropped. My mystery man was standing shirtless, covered in sawdust and sweat. Taking a deep breath, I tried to calm myself as he walked towards us using a blue rag to wipe his face.

"You have a kid?"

"You throw a hammer at us, and the first thing you say is 'You have a kid?'"

"Yeah—I mean, um—I'm sorry. No one is ever here. Throwing tools is how I work." A drop of sweat trailed down his neck, over his perfectly sculpted torso, and into the band of his underwear that were sticking out just above his ripped blue jeans. *Holy shit.* He cleared his throat and our eyes met. The corner of his lip curled up as he smirked at me. "Hey, my eyes are up here. Quit checking me out like I'm not standing here. I feel so used," he said sarcastically.

Blood rushed to my cheeks. "Oh, shut up. I'm just trying to figure out why you tried to kill us. Why aren't you wearing a shirt?"

"I didn't try to kill you or her. It's hot—I'm sweaty. I don't like wearing shirts when I work. Now answer my question—you have a kid?"

Setting Olivia back down in the grass, I placed my hand on my hip. "She's not mine. She's my friend's little girl. Even if she was––why would it interest you?"

"Because you interest me. What friend? Derek's wife?"

Oh? I interest him? Ignoring my thoughts, I gently nodded towards the barn. "Yeah, she's inside going over designs with some guy."

"Logan never said anything to me about that."

"Well, she's here and I came with her."

"I see that."

As I turned around to check on Olivia, she tripped over a root, almost hitting her head on the trunk of the tree. My mystery man reacted quicker than me, and swooped her up into the air. She squealed with delight, as if she didn't almost eat a face full of tree bark. Wrapping her chubby hands around his neck, she laid her head on his shoulder and closed her eyes in the bright sun.

Tick tock. Tick tock. Watching him hold her was like an alarm on my biological clock. Needing to gain control of my situation, I reached for Olivia, but he shrugged me off.

"She's fine, don't fuss over her. You know, I'm glad you came with Derek's wife today."

"Derek's wife has a name. It's Erin." Staring at him, I try to figure out how he knows Derek, but not Erin, especially since she's the one ordering the furniture.

"She's Mrs. Whitt on all of my orders, so I just refer to her as Derek's wife. We've never properly met. I tend to stay busy in the barn."

A fog took over my mind as I pictured him shirtless, working in the barn with drops of sweat rolling down his back. I must have spaced out a little too long, because he awkwardly cleared his throat, which caused me to jump a few inches from the ground. "Shit! Sorry, I was just—"

"No worries." Laughing, he raked his free hand through his sweaty locks, slicking them back out of his face. "I'm glad you came with Erin today. I wanted to see you again. Things between us didn't end the way I wanted them to."

"No? How did you want it to end?" *Please say it ends with me under you! Jesus, where are my thoughts?* Swallowing, I brushed my hair from my face, trying to gain control of my crazy mind.

"Well for starters, I would have told you my name. Maybe asked you on a date?"

Grabbing the diaper bag, I slung it over my shoulder and started walking back towards the office with him following behind me. "What's your name?"

"Alexander, but you can call me Lex."

"Alright Lex, what would we do on this date you speak of?"

"It depends. When can I pick you up?" Lex ran his fingers through his hair again as I took Olivia from him. She shifted on my shoulder a little before falling back to sleep.

I scoffed as I shook my head, "You're very sure of yourself."

"Only with you. Now, what time?" *I doubt it's just with me. I bet he's this way with most women.*

Like perfectly timed clockwork, Erin walked out of the office, jumping into a conversation I shouldn't even be having. "What time for what?"

"I was asking what time Indie would like me to pick her up for our date." Lex said, nodding toward me with a huge grin plastered across his face. *Fucker.*

"Lex asked me out on a date. I haven't given him an answer yet." I explained to Erin.

Erin looked back and forth between the two of us. She nodded toward the car and I followed her with Olivia still sound asleep on my shoulder. Once she had the baby secured in her car seat she pulled me to the side.

"He's the guy from the bar, isn't he?"

"Yeah."

"And I take it you're going to say yes."

"I don't know." Twisting a few strands of my hair in my fingers I looked back over my shoulder towards Lex. He was leaning against the barn with his long legs stretched out in front of him.

"Is this fun or something else?" Erin questioned.

"Fun? I just met him. Maybe having a friend here would be a good idea."

"And what am I?"

"You're my friend. I'm just saying—maybe making more friends would be nice."

"Just be careful." Sighing, she hopped into the driver's seat. *She isn't happy with my decision, but she rarely is anymore. I'm not her. Being a wife and mom isn't something that is written in my future. I've accepted it, and I hope she can too.*

As I walked back towards Lex, I only had one thought. *He has my attention and I know if I don't give in I'm never going to get him out of my head.*

Lex pushed himself off the barn and stood with his arms crossed over his chest, his face hidden by a shadow. *I wonder what he's thinking. It's so hard for me to read him.* Right on cue, as if he knew I was lost in thought about him, he cleared his throat.

Blue eyes caught me with their gaze and I froze as he took a step towards me. "I'm going to steal you away for a couple of hours tomorrow. I'll pick you up around one."

I haven't even given him an answer yet. "I never said yes."

"You wouldn't have walked all the way back over here just to tell me no."

He's right, but I'm not about to admit it. I'm pissed. If he wants to take me out on a date, he should try asking me and actually letting me answer him. "For future reference, most women don't like dictators." *This was a bad idea.* I turned around to walk back toward the car when his fingers laced in mine, halting me in my tracks.

"I keep messing this up," he said sounding disappointed.

"You really do."

"Will you go out with me tomorrow? We could go for lunch— just something small."

"I'd love to. All you had to do was ask." I said with a smile. "If you don't want to pick me up, I could meet you somewhere."

"No, I'll come get you." His thumb brushed against my skin as he slowly pulled me back toward him. Wrapping a hand around my neck he softly kissed my lips before pressing his forehead to mine. "Why is talking to you so hard?"

"I don't know. I didn't think it was."

"You're so different."

Placing a soft kiss on his cheek, I turned around and walked back to the car. *Am I really that hard to talk to? There's just something different about him. He's not like the other guys I've dated.* Sliding into my seat, I clicked my seatbelt into place after shutting the door.

Turning down the radio, Erin twisted in her seat to get a better look at me. "So, what did he say?"

"He's picking me up tomorrow for a lunch date."

"Really?" Her eyes flash towards the rearview mirror as she slowly backed out of the parking spot.

"Erin, what do you know about him?" I asked sincerely.

"Nothing. I mean—I knew Logan had a business partner, but I had no idea he was that hot."

"What?"

"I mean—I didn't know he worked with Logan. I also didn't realize how good-looking he was. Jesus, Indie—you're in over your head."

"You think so?"

"Yeah, I do. I see the way you look at him, but what you don't see, is how he looks at you."

"And how exactly does he look at me?"

"Like you're the only person in front of him. His eyes don't leave you, but it's just fun, right? Nothing more than friends." She glanced at me out of the corner of her eye as she pulled onto the street. *I know what she's insinuating, but she's wrong. It's not what she thinks it is.*

"Yeah. Friends." I confirmed.

The drive back to the house was quiet. Neither of us said anything more about Lex or my impending date.

Chapter

Four

Nervousness. It's such an odd feeling for me. When it comes to my life, I try my best to keep everything in a certain order because I don't like feeling this way. When I get nervous, I have panic attacks. My stay here was supposed to be a break from everything and yet—here I stand, in front of the mirror, feeling nervous. I barely ate any of my dinner last night. I mostly picked at my food while Derek and Erin argued about some football coach. This morning I drank my coffee and grazed on a donut. My appetite has escaped me, and now I'm left nervous…on an empty stomach.

The doorbell rang, letting me know it was time for me to come down from my tower. I didn't have time to change my clothes, but I did at least take the time to flat iron my hair and throw some lip-gloss on. I looked myself over once more, grabbed my clutch, and headed down the stairs.

When I got downstairs, Lex was sitting awkwardly in the living room with Erin and Derek. Whatever secrets were between him and Derek were creating pliable tension. Neither one looked at the other. Poor Erin was trying her best to hold a conversation, but both men only grunted in response.

Standing, Lex walked over to me, wrapping one arm around my waist. "You ready?" he asked.

The nervousness I had just a few moments ago disappeared as he pulled me toward him. His hand rested so gently on my hip, I barely noticed it. "I think so."

"Alright, let's go." Linking my fingers with his, he led me from the room and out the front door to his black truck. I hopped into the passenger seat with a little help from him. It's not that I couldn't get in on my own, it's just that his truck was so high from the ground there's no classy way for me to do it without a boost from him.

Country music spilled from the speakers surrounding us as we drove along the highway. I crumpled my nose at the cracks in the voice accompanying the guitar chords being plucked ferociously.

Seeing my expression, Lex asked, "I take it this isn't something you normally listen to?"

"It's not that it's bad—it's just not my normal cup of tea."

"You probably listen to the Backstreet Boys all day, dancing around in your oversized pajamas."

Laughing, I shook my head. "Don't knock the Backstreet Boys! And just so you know, I don't wear oversized pajamas. I just prefer different music—something I can dance to."

"You can dance to this." he quipped.

"I don't see how that's possible. I can't picture me standing in any kind of line repeating steps. Even the Electric Slide turns me away. I'm awful at anything requiring strategic moves."

Lex turned off the highway onto a smaller road and slowed the truck to a stop. Turning up the radio, he stepped out and walked around the truck. Looking around, all I could see were cornfields surrounding us. *What the hell is he doing?* A sudden tap on my window caught my attention. Rolling down my window, I leaned my arm against the door and bat my eyelashes at him.

"Can I help you, sir? It seems my date has stepped out for the minute. I'm sure he will be right back."

Chuckling to himself, he opens my door. "Come on, city girl. There are lessons to be learned."

"Like what?" I asked in confusion.

"You'll see."

Slipping my hand into his, I hopped down from the truck. He led me around the truck to the side of the road where the gravel hit the dry, red clay dirt. Though I could still hear the music playing inside the truck. A male voice came across the radio, making a few announcements before mentioning the next song. *Take Your Time* by Sam Hunt began to play. At first, I'm taken back by the way he talks over the music before letting out some serious notes. *This isn't like the last song we heard.*

Lex slowly pulled me toward him as we began to sway to the music. He was light on his feet and I found myself moving with ease along with him. Raising my hand in the air he spun me around a few times before wrapping one arm around my waist, pulling me back to him. Resting his forehead against mine, he mouthed the words to the song as I found myself completely lost in the moment. He spun me around, guiding me back to the truck. When the song ended he continued to hold me close to him. His nose was just a few inches from mine as he whispered, "I knew you could dance."

When I came down from the cloud I found myself floating on, I softly smiled at him. "I'm almost certain you were the one dancing. I was just following along."

"It still counts. Come on, we have things to do."

Slipping from his grasp, I hopped back into my seat and watched him as he walked around the truck in his tight blue jeans. Greeting me with a lopsided grin, he started the truck and pulled back onto the road. Music continued to play on the radio, though I paid no attention to it. Instead, my mind drifted off with thoughts of what it might be like to live here. *There's no pressure here. Everything seems slower, sweeter.*

We were driving down a gravel road when Lex pulled the truck to a stop next to a very worn-looking wooden bench. With a grin, he turned off the truck, jumped out, and started grabbing stuff from the back. Not wanting to miss out on whatever he had planned, I opened my door and jumped down. The red clay dirt was barely covered by the sparse grass trying its best to grow on the top of the hill. I immediately noticed the worn path leading through the trees and I couldn't help but look down at my shoes. *I have a feeling I will need to wear something other than flats or sandals if I'm going to keep hanging out with this boy.*

"So, what's the plan?" I asked, leaning against the tailgate. My eyes focused in on the plastic box and two fishing poles. "Tell me this isn't happening?"

"Calm down. You're acting like I'm going to make you use worms."

"Um, isn't that how you catch a fish? Worm on a hook?"

"You can, but I prefer to use lures. What kind of fancy life have you led, lady? We're going fishing. We aren't mud wrestling."

Disdain. It's the only word that comes to mind when I think of standing near water for hours, trying to catch a fish. *Bugs, dirt, and sweat do not sound appealing. I need to look at this from a different perspective. There's a cute guy, whom I'm genuinely interested in, wanting to take me to a private beach. That sounds so much better.* I tried to convince myself.

Lex tucked a blanket and the tackle box under one arm, while holding the poles in the other as he started off down the worn path, motioning for me to follow.

His tight, dark blue jeans held my attention as we carefully made our way down the hill. I couldn't help but think, *It's almost as though they were perfectly crafted to enhance the curve of his ass.* Using low-hanging branches from the trees around us as support, I was able to make it down the dirt path without falling on my ass. When I reached the bottom I turned around, glancing at the hill behind me, *I hope I don't fall going back up.*

Lex laid the blanket on the bank, as the water lapped at the edge, softly kissing rocks and debris from fallen trees. I watched him as he opened the tackle box and carefully attached weird-looking feathers with silver ovals on them to the end of the fishing line. He tied intricate knots before tugging on the lures to make sure they were secure.

"Do you know how to cast?"

"Not with this pole. Do you know how to ballroom dance?"

"Yes, and that's an odd question."

"Are you being serious right now? You really know how to ballroom dance?"

"Yes. Now do you know how to cast?" Arching his left eyebrow, he looked me over. "Sandals? I thought we talked about this."

"Don't look at me like that. I didn't know where you were going to take me. Besides, they're comfortable. And for your information, my brother took me fishing once. He taught me how to cast, but we used worms. My pole also had a push button thingy."

Rubbing the back of his neck he flashed me a grin. "You're full of surprises, aren't you? Come here, city girl, I'll show you how to cast with this. It doesn't have a 'button thingy.'"

"Stop calling me that. I'll have you know I wasn't always a city girl."

"No? What kind of girl were you?"

"Um, I was a classy girl. My family belongs to a very wealthy country club in New Hampshire." Laughing, I covered my face with my hands. "God, that sounded worse than I thought."

"I don't even know how to respond to that." Laughing, he handed me one of the rods and led me to a flat spot at the edge of the bank. "You want to try and cast toward that darker water out there…by that cluster of rocks. The bass love to hang out there. The idea is to catch one without getting your line tangled. This is a spinning rod. Flip this little round piece of metal up, while keeping your thumb on the line. Pull it back. When you're ready, bring the pole back around and let go of the line. Once it hits the water, flip this piece back down. Okay?"

A deer in headlights. That's exactly how I felt and looked. I didn't understand any of what he said, so I just stood there, staring at him, blinking like a fool. Lex stepped behind me. Reaching one of his arms around me, while gripping the fishing pole in the other, his hands softly positioned mine where they needed to be. I could feel the warmth from his body through my thin t-shirt and the stubble of his jaw brushing against my ear. *It's so hard to concentrate when he's touching me like this.*

"Hold it like this—now put your thumb right here and don't move it until you're ready to cast."

I swallowed and took a deep breath in through my nose, trying to calm myself down. Instead, I ended up breathing in the scent of his cologne, mixed with sweat. *Jesus. I'm in so much trouble.* I was at a loss with what else to do to ease my nerves. Slowly letting go of my hands, he stepped to the side. I did exactly as he said and my line flew out across the water, landing about ten feet from the rocks. "Lex, I did it!"

"Of course you did, I'm a great teacher. Now slowly reel it back in and do it again. I like to jerk the line a bit, but you don't have to."

Looking over my shoulder, I flashed him the biggest smile I could muster. *I can't believe I'm enjoying this. Erin is never going to believe me when I tell her I went fishing.* Lex walked up beside me and cast his line. I tried my best to mimic his moves, casting a few more times before I watched his pole bend as he reeled in a fish. Holding it up in the air, he tried to hand it to me.

"Do you want to pull the hook out?"

"What? No! That's so disgusting. My skin is cringing just from thinking about how grotesque it is."

"It's just a fish."

"Exactly! I'm not touching it. Come near me and I will start walking back to Erin's. No—just no."

Chuckling, Lex popped the hook out and released the fish back into the water. "In all my life, I've never met someone who is afraid of a little bass."

"Little? That was not little. A goldfish is little. That fish was at least six inches."

"I caught one at least ten inches long the other day."

"That, my friend, is a lie. You're male—lying about size is in your genetics."

"So, what you're implying is I don't know what ten inches is?"

"Listen, when a guy says ten inches you subtract at least four. For some reason, you all think five inches is equivalent to nine inches. Measurement isn't your greatest strength as a species."

Lex stood perfectly still, staring at me for a few seconds before gathering up the blanket and tackle box. I watched as his muscles flexed while he bundled the poles, along with everything else under his arms. "I have half a mind to show you what ten inches really looks like. Come on, city girl."

Are we still talking about the fish? I watched in confusion as he walked back up the path. *Are we done already? What was the point of all of this?*

I was a few steps behind him when Lex pulled down the tailgate, dropping everything with a loud bang on the bed of his truck. The mid-day sun reflected off the paint, creating a glare that messed with my view. As I came around the back of the truck I noticed one hand tucked in the front pocket of his blue jeans. With a quick flash of his teeth he motioned me to come to him.

The gravel crunched under my feet as I approached him. My palms began to sweat and the hair on my arm rose. It was a welcome reminder to not get in over my head. *I need to keep everything sorted clearly in my mind. This is me letting go a little bit—it's not serious. Though there's something about him that pulls me in. I need to figure out what it is and get it out of my system.*

My feet stopped abruptly in front of his worn tan boots. He cleared his throat and our eyes met. Giving me a wink, he slid his arms around my waist, picking me up, and setting me on the bed of the truck. "I don't like company. I like to do things on my own, work things out for myself, and yet here I am, trying to figure out a way to make you want to spend the day with me. Dancing didn't work. Fishing didn't work. This is new to me—help me out here."

"I'm just having fun. I needed a break from everything. I needed new scenery and a place to breathe. My place back in New York was suffocating me. Now I'm here. That's what this is. It's just me breathing in some fresh air for the summer. I wasn't expecting you—you weren't on my approved list of activities."

"Lists, measurements, and bad pick-up lines. I need more to work with than that. What is it that you do back in that city of yours?"

Do I tell him the truth? New York is no longer my home. The fact is, I don't even have a home right now. Does that make me homeless? God knows I can't say that. He would walk out on me. Instead I tell the truth mixed with a lie. "I make things beautiful. I turn vacant spaces into works of art and hopefully leave people breathless."

"Now that's something I can agree with."

"What?"

"Well you left me breathless the moment you sat down next to me at the bar. You looked so out of place, I just had to talk to you. You weren't in my plans either, but I'm happy I saw you that night."

Not knowing what to say, I started fidgeting with the hairband on my wrist. Just as I started to pull my hair up, he stopped me. "Leave it down, you look beautiful." My hair slipped from my hands as he swirled a few strands around his finger.

Something changed in the air around us and suddenly I was aware of how close he was to me. His body stiffened as his face stopped inches from mine. *Whatever I feel, he feels it too.* Clearing my throat, I tucked my hair behind my ear. "What are we doing?"

"Hell if I know. All I know is we have the summer to figure it out."

Lex softly pressed his lips to mine. They barely touched for a brief second. His thumb brushed my bottom lip as he gave me a devilish look. "Get in the truck." I swear he smirked at me as he held out his hand, helping me down. I'm not one to be told what to do, but I can't help the way my body pulls to him. *Lust. That's what this is. Lust I can handle, love is something completely different.*

The truck rumbled to life as Lex stared at me. "Where are we going, baby?"

Clicking my seatbelt into place, I gave him a soft smile. "Baby? I'm nobody's baby. I'm a grown woman, completely competent in taking care of myself."

"My apologies. Now, can you tell me where we are going?"

"You said you were going to feed me. Take me to lunch."

"Yes ma'am." Normally being called ma'am would irritate me, I'm not old enough to be called a ma'am—that's a lie. I just don't feel old enough to be called ma'am. That title is reserved for my mother and her snobby friends. Lex, however, could call me ma'am anytime he wants. I loved the way it rolled off his tongue in his southern accent.

My eyes followed the scenery as he turned onto the highway. I thought we were farther from the city, but it didn't take long to get back to a bustling suburb. It's not a city like I'm used to—it moves to a slower beat, though I'm starting to fall in love with it. Lex parked the truck in front of a red brick building with *Sam's* written in bold, yellow letters above the front doors. Raising my brow, I questioned Lex's choice for lunch. Laughing, he jumped out of the truck and motioned for me to follow. As I stepped out of the truck, he grabbed my hand and led me toward the front of the restaurant.

"What is this place?" I asked.

In true smartass fashion, he replied, "It's a restaurant. They make great burgers."

"I'm guessing a salad isn't an option?"

"Why wouldn't it be? We aren't savages you know. If you want rabbit food, they will make you that too."

Pushing open the glass door, we stepped inside. Large wooden tables sat scattered throughout the restaurant. Almost every table was bar height, while shorter booths lined the red brick walls. Different sports were playing on the televisions scattered around the place. We were shown to a table and as soon as I hopped up onto the chair a pretty girl, with blonde hair pulled back in twists, walked over to take our order. She blinked a couple of times at Lex before saying anything, although he was too busy looking over the beer list to even notice. *I wonder how often that happens.*

"Y'all ready to order?" Her drawl was slow and sweet.

"Um, I think we will need a minute. Can I get some water?"

She shot me an icy glare, followed by a fake smile. "Sure—and for you?" She bat her eyelashes once again at Lex. This time he noticed. His eyes went wide and he pointed to the menu. "Yuenglings. Draft, please."

Nodding her head, she sauntered away swinging her hips a little too much for my liking.

"I think she likes you."

Rolling his eyes, he ran his hands through his blonde locks. "I thought she was going to lick me."

I let out a laugh. "Lick you? Just how many times have random women licked you?"

"One thing at a time. What kind of rabbit food are you going to order?"

"Just a salad. Don't dodge my questions."

"Fine. It happened once at a bar. Now leave it."

"Um, okay." My mouth opened to add a little bit more to my lacking statement, but the waitress walked over with our drinks, silencing me when she tapped her pen to her pad of paper.

"What can I get y'all?" she asked.

"I'll take the American cheeseburger with a slice of cheddar and some fries." Pointing to me, he said, "She wants rabbit food."

Glaring at Lex, I corrected him. "May I have a salad, please? Vinaigrette dressing, on the side, with extra cucumbers, please."

"Sure. I'll put it right in." The waitress flashed Lex another smile before walking away with her hips swinging in tune to the music being played overhead.

"She likes you."

"No, she likes the way I look. She doesn't know me."

I started to counter his argument when a sweet lady sitting at the table beside us threw a balled-up napkin at him, before quickly looking away. Lex looked over his shoulder and a grin suddenly spread across his face when he found the culprit. "Bobbi? I'm not saying it was you, but the only place that could have come from is your table."

Feigning innocence, she replied, "Wasn't me." It didn't last long before she started laughing so hard the table shook in front of her. The small bits of silver in her short curly hair made her eyes shine just a little bit brighter as she smiled sweetly.

"Hey, how's the shop?" The gentleman sitting across from her asked as he turned to face Lex, completely ignoring the woman, who I assume is his wife.

"Good. Staying busy. Lots of hours, but at least it's steady."

"That's good to hear. Lots of things are slowing down these days. I'm glad you guys are doing well. That's all you can ask for."

"You're right about that."

The lady stood from the table and walked toward me, holding out her hand, as her husband slipped some cash on the table. I couldn't help but notice her beautiful silver bracelet glittering on her wrist. "I'm Bobbi. This is my husband, Joe. Alexander has helped us with our house some." *I'm not sure what it is about her, but I like her.*

"Has he? It's nice to meet you both. I'm Indie."

"Well, that's a beautiful name."

"Thank you. I like to think so."

"Well, you two go ahead and eat. We have some running around to do. It's been nice seeing you. Tell Logan we said hello."

"Will do, Miss Bobbi." Lex stood, shaking their hands before sitting back down across from me. *Miss Bobbi? How is it that she gets a Miss and I'm a ma'am?*

"I'm intrigued by you. First the waitress, and now a random lady is fawning over you."

"Who? Bobbi? She's not fawning—she's just sweet. It's who she is. I helped Joe with their deck last summer. He also commissioned us to make her an armoire for her birthday. They're just good people."

"And the waitress?" I quipped.

"I can't help it if she notices how amazing I look." Leaning back in his seat, he folded his hands behind his head as he gave me a little wink.

"Wow, you're such an ass."

"Ass? I'm not an ass. I just like getting a rise out of you."

"I don't know if I should smack you or kiss you."

"Then it's working." Grinning, Lex pulled his phone out of his back pocket and laid it on the table.

Rolling my eyes, I took a sip of my drink. The waitress brought our meals over to the table, giving Lex another smile as she put his plate in front of him. Taking a bite of my salad, I watched him eat his food through hooded eyes. *He's so incredibly handsome. Maybe I'm the only one that sees him like this. That would explain why he doesn't have a girlfriend.*

My thoughts were tumbling in my mind when my phone buzzed in my pocket. It was a message from Erin asking if I was coming back today. I text her back letting her know that I planned on it, but right now I was on a date and she needed to stay out of it. All I got in response was a series of dots. Rolling my eyes, I tossed my phone in my clutch.

"Was that Derek's wife?"

"Her name is Erin—and yes. She wanted to make sure I wasn't in danger. I told her I was having some fun and that I'd see her later."

"You're with me—that's definite danger." Running his hands through his hair, he gave me a devilish smirk.

"Has anyone ever told you how cocky you are?"

"Once again, just with you. Tell me why I'm fun."

"Tell me why you asked me out."

"I already told you—you were different. Now answer my question."

Sighing, I picked at my napkin before looking him in the eyes. "You make me smile. That's not easily done."

He sat quietly for a few minutes, looking me over. Just as he opened his mouth, his phone buzzed on the table. Setting down his drink, he reached for it as it went off again. 'Evil Bitch' lit up on the screen. Worry creased his brow as his fingers scrolled across the screen, ignoring the call. Closing his eyes, he let out a long sigh as it lit up again. This time I was able to make out the words, 'Need a ride' before his fingers swiped the message away.

"Indie, as much fun as this is, I need to head back to work. I told Logan lunch, and we've gone way past that, and that's not like me. I keep my word, and I just—we need to go."

I was lost in my head as he paid for our meal and led me back to his truck. *This has gone from the best date I have ever had, to the worst, in just a few split seconds. I'm not sure who 'Evil Bitch' is, but I know she's the real reason our date is over.*

Neither one of us said a word during the drive back to Erin's. He pulled up the long drive and put his truck in park. Letting out a deep sigh, I unclicked my seatbelt and started to open my door when he stopped me.

"Look at me. Please?"

Ignoring his words, I focused on the scenery outside my window. "I had a nice time. Thank you for lunch."

"Indie—look at me." Turning to face him, I was met with deep blue eyes filled with sadness. *I wish I could take whatever it is that's hurting him away.* His hand grasped mine and the current in the air changed once again. Everything suddenly felt so alive. I was frozen in place, afraid to move, because one spark may set off a chain of reactions I couldn't stop. The vein in his neck was pulsing, indicating his heart was beating just as fast as mine—maybe even faster. His tongue slowly darted out, wetting his bottom lip, and I found myself mimicking his actions.

"Lex—"

"Don't." His strong hands wrapped around the back of my neck, pulling my body to his. My lips found his and sparks flew. Every question, every thought, it all disappeared. My focus was now on getting closer to him. As I climbed over the console separating the seats, and into his lap, my ass pressed against the steering wheel causing the horn to blare.

Laughing, Lex reclined his seat just enough to let me straddle him. His palms slid over my ass, while I pressed my body closer to his. My fingers knotted in his hair as our tongues danced among our heavy breaths. A soft moan fell from my lips as his hand slid under my shirt, palming my breast. His thumb gently brushed against my hardening nipple through the silky material of my bra. *Fuck.* My hands barely touched the firm skin of his stomach before he grabbed my arms, completely stopping all of our movements.

"As badly as I want this, I don't want to do this in your friend's driveway. I might be an asshole, but I'm not that kind of an asshole."

Nodding my head, I pressed my forehead against his as I caught my breath. *Holy. Shit. That was incredible. I'm going to need a lot more than a hot shower to calm myself down from this.* Climbing back into my seat, I grabbed my clutch from the floorboard. When I looked up he was already walking around to the passenger side of the truck. Opening my door, he took my hand, helped me down, and walked me to the front door.

Twirling a strand of my hair between his fingers, he pressed his forehead to mine. "What am I going to do with you?"

"I don't know," I replied breathlessly.

"Neither do I."

I wanted to ask him so many questions. *Why do his eyes look so sad? Is the person that messaged him the shadow I saw the other night at the bar?* One minute he's so cocky and self-assured, the next minute he looks lost—almost pained. He was all over the place with his emotions and I felt dizzy just trying to keep up with him.

Giving me a soft kiss, he turned and jogged back to his truck, leaving me completely befuddled, standing in my friend's driveway.

Not wanting to watch him drive away, I stepped into the house and quietly shut the door behind me. Erin was in the kitchen where I could hear Olivia's soft giggles. I made it to the first step before I heard her call out behind me.

"So…the fun?"

"It was fun, but I don't know. Maybe it's not as fun as I thought. He's so confusing—I think someone hurt him."

"What do you mean?"

"Nothing—never mind. I'm going to take a shower and maybe nap for a bit. Do we have plans for tonight?"

"Nothing big. Derek is stuck at the hospital, so it's just you, me, and Olivia for a while."

Nodding my head, I headed up the stairs. It's not until I reach the door to my bedroom that I realize she probably didn't hear my head nod.

What is Lex doing to me?

Chapter Five

Four days had passed since the last time I saw Lex. If I had his number I would have called him, but I wasn't smart enough to ask for it. I'm still confused on how things were left between us, but I figured he would have come over or something—maybe even try to get my number from Derek. Instead, I've been left wondering if I'll ever see him again.

Erin is insistent that I 'get back out there,' so tonight we are going to play some pool. Clarissa will be here in a little bit to watch Olivia, and Derek made Erin promise not to drink too much, but I refused to promise anything. *I need fun. I want to have some 'let my hair down, crazy dancing' kind of fun, so if I need a few drinks to open-up—then so be it.*

"How much longer are you going to lie on the couch and mope? What happened to just having fun? Besides, I thought relationships were out of the question?"

"One lunch date doesn't count as a relationship—don't make this into something it isn't. I'm not moping either...I'm just resting before we go out because I plan on dancing my ass off."

"You'll need to get dressed then—it's almost seven o'clock. Clarissa will be here in thirty minutes."

"Shit! Are you serious? Why didn't you tell me it was so late?"

"I did—just now." Erin grinned as if this situation was hilarious. I returned her gaze with a deadly glare. *I can't believe I didn't notice the time.* Jumping up from the couch, I ran up the first set of stairs, but after almost dying from a heart attack I decided to walk the rest.

I rummaged through my clothes, until I found the perfect outfit. It screamed single, independent female. After pulling on a teal colored, silk dress with some black sandals that wrapped up my calves, tying just below my knee, I looked myself over in the mirror. I pull the hairband from my hair and messy waves cascaded around my shoulders. Using a little bit of dry shampoo, I worked my hair into soft, subtle waves and pinned it to one side. Just in case the odds of Lex being there tonight are in my favor, I want him to see what he's missing. *Hell, maybe I'll find someone else to scratch the itch he's created.*

By the time I got downstairs, Erin was already giving Clarissa the same lecture as the other night. *I wonder how many times the poor girl has had to listen to that exact same spiel.* Deciding to wait for Erin, I leaned against the wall by the front door when Derek stepped out of the kitchen.

"Wow."

"You think? That's what I was going for."

Derek scrubbed his hand over the top of his head before letting out a sigh. "If Erin went out like that—I don't think we'd make it anywhere."

"We wouldn't go where?" Erin asked, as she walked around the corner with her purse slung over her shoulder, stopping dead in her tracks when she saw me. "Holy shit, Indie."

"Do you think I should change?"

"No! If I still had 'fuck me' legs like that, I would show them off every chance I got."

Derek wrapped his arm around Erin and softly kissed her neck. "Baby, you have 'fuck me' everything." She giggled as she leaned into him and placed a kiss on his lips. As sweet as they looked, I didn't want to see where this conversation was going.

"Are you set then?" Looking around the room, I tried not to make eye contact with whatever make-out session they were currently engaged in.

"Yeah, Clarissa has our numbers. Come on—let's get you to the bar so you can have your fun." Erin looped her arm through mine as we walked out the front door, ready for a night of dancing.

"This place seems different from the last time." I yelled to Erin over the loud music, before taking a sip of the third drink Derek just brought me.

"Yeah, it can get crazy in here on Saturday nights. Just wait until the band starts to play."

"Who are they?"

"I don't know. It's a bunch of younger kids playing older rock songs. They're pretty good."

"Young? The lead singer looks like he's at least twenty-five."

"Yeah—well, I'm a mom, that makes me old." The loud song playing through the speakers, ended perfectly halfway through Erin's sentence, so she ended up yelling loudly across the bar. I found it to be hilarious. She, however, didn't and ended up throwing a wadded up napkin at me. Unfortunately for her, she missed me and hit a brunette with short, curly hair behind us in the shoulder.

Turning around, the woman gave Erin a scornful glare, but she pointed at me as if it was all my doing. The woman planted her hand on her hip and stared at me as if I owed her something. "You going to apologize?" she asked, her high-pitched voice scratching against my skin like broken glass.

"For?" *Now is not the time to be a smartass, but it's in my nature. I can't help it.*

She spun back around and whispered to a rather big guy perched beside her on a barstool. He brushed her off, but when she wouldn't stop tugging on his cut-off shirt he turned towards me. Pointing at me he asked, "Her?"

"Yeah, she's the one that did it."

Glaring at the curly haired woman, my eyes raked over her. She was wearing a denim skirt, barely long enough to cover her ass, and a green plaid button up shirt that she had tied into a knot just above her belly button. I couldn't help but wonder if she might be the local town whore. Taking a sip of my drink, I offered them both a smile with just a hint of sassiness. "I didn't do anything. Why don't you sit back down, and go back to hooking, or whatever it is that you do? I'm sure if you play nice with him he'll give you a good tip."

Erin gasped as my name barely fell from her lips. "Indie—shut up."

"You should listen to your friend. Apologize to my girl here and then turn around and shut-up."

"No."

"Now, normally when a pretty little thing like you walks into a place like this, I can't help but wonder what she's up to—it seems to me that you want to cause trouble. Maybe you need someone to remind you of your place. Maybe you like when people get a little rough with you. Be careful, sweetheart, you're a tiny little thing. I wouldn't want you getting hurt over something so small." Setting down his beer, he stood, knocking over his barstool. The air in the room stilled as he stepped toward me.

"I may be pretty, but I'm not little." Crossing my arms over my chest, I glared at the man now towering over me. Erin kicked me under the table, but I ignored it.

"That's not how I see it. Now, you've gone and thrown something at her, are you going to apologize or not?"

"Yeah, about that—I didn't do it, so you can go back to doing whatever it was you were doing before you decided to block our table with your shadow." Erin kicked me again, but this time the pain registered with my mind. Reaching down under the table, I rubbed my shin. *Her boots are going to leave a mark.*

"Who the hell do you think you are, missy?"

"Someone who doesn't want to talk to you. Seriously, don't you have someone else to go intimidate into an apology for something they didn't do? You need to fuck off." I have always had a hard time knowing when to shut-up. As usual, my mouth had gotten me into trouble—but this time was different. Normally, I'm escorted from the bar, or someone pulls me away. Not this time. This time my head flew backwards and my body crumpled to the floor. Being a fan of classic black and white films, I often wondered if being backhanded felt as dramatic as it looked. Unfortunately for me, I now knew the answer.

I was pushing myself up from the floor, when two chairs in front of me were knocked out of the way, and a pair of worn, tan boots leapt over me. I heard a growl, followed by a loud crash. Covering my head with my arms, I watched as Lex fell to the ground beside me. *Fuck. This.* Standing up, I turned around to face the asshole who was now bragging to his friends about how he 'handled' the situation. Unbeknownst to him, he hadn't handled anything.

"What the hell is your problem? Who the fuck hits a woman? Didn't your mom teach you any manners?" I must have hit a nerve because he lunged toward me. The year of self-defense classes I took was now paying off. As I bend my leg, kneeing him in the groin, I slammed the palm of my hand in an upward thrust against his nose. He fell to the floor with a loud moan, gripping his face. When one of the asshole's friends started to make a nasty comment about me, Erin lunged at him. Derek was quick to stop her as he wrapped both arms around her waist, carrying her out of the bar. I was ready to let loose as I pulled my arm back in hopes of connecting with the other asshole's face, when suddenly, I was lifted from the floor.

"Alright, Mohamad Ali—it's time to go. I think they got the message loud and clear. You're tough. They won't mess with you again."

I yelped in shock as Lex tossed me over his shoulder. I smacked his back a few times, yelling for him to put me down, but he didn't listen. Instead, he laughed, as he carried me out of the bar. He didn't put me down until he reached his truck and opened the tailgate. Setting me down on the bed of the truck, he looked me over. He sighed as his fingers gently brushed the skin under my left eye. I pulled away, cringing from the stinging pain.

"That's going to bruise." When I looked up at him, I noticed a small trickle of blood coming from his bottom lip. Using his tongue, he carefully probed the cut, while shaking his head. "Who are you? I've never seen someone so tiny try to take on someone at least twice their size."

"I didn't need you to rescue me. I can take care of myself."

"I saw that," he retorted. Sighing, he ran his hands through his hair. "Some girls like to be saved."

"Yeah, well, I'm not one of them. What the hell were you thinking?"

"I don't know. All of a sudden I felt this intense rage. Who the fuck hits a girl? I thought I was protecting you."

"Some kind of rage that was. He knocked you on your ass."

"I noticed."

"Lex, I'm not a damsel in distress and you are not a knight in shining armor." Sighing, I stared back into solemn eyes. "Why didn't you call or stop by? I haven't heard from you in four days. I was enjoying my drink when some snotty bitch decided to tell the Hulk I started shit with her. I stood my ground and the next thing I know I'm landing on the floor. Then I watched as you landed next to me."

"I'm sorry—I made a mistake. This is new to me, remember? I have no clue what I'm doing."

"That's obvious."

"You're mad."

"Shouldn't I be? Tonight has been a complete nightmare."

Gently lifting my chin with his fingers, Lex softly pressed his lips to mine. The slight taste of copper hit my tongue as my hands wrapped around his neck. Pressing his forehead to mine, he slowly untangled himself from my arms. Flipping one of my hands over, he inspected it thoroughly, before doing the same to my other hand. "You're bleeding."

Pulling my hand from his, I looked down at my palm. "No—it's not mine. I think I might have broken his nose."

"Jesus, woman. Remind me to never piss you off."

The gravel crunched and I looked over to see Derek walking toward us, looking rather irritated. *Fuck.*

"Oh shit!" Lex caught my gaze and walked toward Derek. I'm not sure what they were saying, but it was obvious that Derek was pissed off. I heard my name being yelled a few times before Derek finally walked away. Lex turned around, tucking his hands into his pocket, and slowly walked back toward me.

"You've gotten yourself into trouble. He's pissed, but I think he's more pissed at his wife for starting all of it. He wanted you to come back with them, but I've convinced him to let you stay with me."

"I don't belong to anyone so you didn't need to convince him."

"I get what you're saying, but let's not ruffle his feathers any more than they already are."

"So now what?"

"Now, you come home with me. You need ice on that before it swells shut." His fingers softly brushed my cheek before he lifted me off the truck and set me back down on the gravel.

"And I get no say in the matter?" I asked, leaning against the truck, tapping my foot.

"Indie, please come home with me. I'm worried about you."

Wanting to avoid a lecture from Derek, I took my chance with Lex. "Okay." Slowly climbing into the passenger seat with a little help from Lex, I made myself comfortable before checking my face in the rearview mirror. My cheekbone was already starting to turn a little purple. *Perfect.* As he slid into his seat I managed to get a better look of his face. His lip was swollen, but it didn't look too bad. He spun the dial on the radio until he found a song he liked, and then gave me a little wink as we turned onto the dimly lit street.

Carefully leaning against the headrest of my seat, I watched him as he drove, tapping the steering wheel with his fingers to the beat of the songs being played. His mouth twitched a couple of times as his tongue brushed against his lower lip. For someone I had just met, he was holding an awful lot of my attention. Instead of wondering what it meant, I focused on the now. *I'm being taking home by an incredibly handsome guy who just happens to make my heart flutter.* The thought had my heart racing. Exhaustion finally began to set in as I blinked my eyes a few times.

"I see your eyes closing on me. Keep those open, okay? We're almost home."

"Okay." My brain didn't fully register what he was saying, but I knew he wanted me to stay awake.

My eyes opened and shut a few more times before I felt the truck come to a stop.

"You still with me?"

"Uh huh," I groggily replied.

Opening my door, Lex lifted me out of the truck and carried me through the front door of a house that looked vaguely familiar. Setting me down on a wooden stool inside his kitchen, he said, "I'm worried about your head. I'm going to set you down for just a second while I grab a flashlight, okay?"

"Uh huh." *I'm not sure what he's worried about. My head doesn't hurt—I'm just tired.* My eyes peered around the room while I waited for him to return. Besides the few dishes in the sink, it didn't look lived in at all. The white cabinets were pristine, along with the white marble countertops. Thin gray and black mosaic tiles lined the wall space between the cabinets and the sink. What caught my attention was the odd shaped faucet. As I stepped down from the stool to take a closer look, I lost my footing and stumbled a bit, catching myself on the counter in front of me. *Maybe I hit my head a little harder than I originally thought.*

"Whoa—I thought I told you to stay," Lex said, rushing to my side.

"No, you said you were going to set me down and you did."

Sighing, Lex picked me up and set me back down on the barstool. "Now I'm telling you to stay."

"Okay."

Shaking his head, Lex turned on the flashlight and had me look directly at him as he checked my eyes. "Your eyes seem okay, but I'm still worried. Looks like we are staying up for a little while. Come on—I'm taking you to bed."

Shit. Just the sound of those words falling from his lips had me clenching my thighs together. *What exactly is he planning on us doing?* "Lex—"

"Don't worry, we'll both keep our clothes on."

"Oh." I went from anxious to disappointed in less than five seconds. Lex wrapped my legs around his waist and lifted me from the stool. Wrapping my arms around his neck I looked him square in the eyes. "My feet work."

"I know. Trust me, if you hadn't hit your head, you'd be walking right now, but I don't want you falling on the stairs."

Nodding, I laid my head on his shoulder as he led us down a dark hallway, up the stairs, and into his bedroom. Soft gray hues mixed with the dark walnut of the exquisitely carved furniture. The lion's feet on the bottom of the dresser reminded me of the furniture at Erin's. "Is everything you touch so beautiful?" It wasn't exactly the question I wanted to ask, but it was the one that came out.

"Only you." he replied. Setting me down on the edge of the bed, he grabbed a blanket off an oversized chair in the corner of the room. Scooting back towards the headboard, I laid my head on the soft, plush pillows. My eyes blinked a few times before I was suddenly sitting up, with Lex staring at me.

"No sleeping. Not yet, anyway. Tell me about you."

"I thought I told you already." Yawning, I stretched my arms above my head before scooting next to Lex. *If I can't lie on the pillow, then I will lay on him.*

"You told me you make things beautiful."

"People pay me to decorate their apartments and condos before they sell them. Well—they used to. I don't do that anymore. I like this furniture. Did you make this too?" Laying my head on his shoulder, I traced the contours of his forearms with my fingers.

"Logan designs it, I build it. He's brilliant."

"How do you know Logan? I mean, he's your boss, right? How did you end up working for him?"

"Logan is my…he's my partner. I've known him for as long as I can remember. I didn't realize you knew him too."

"Oh, no—I don't. I met him the other morning. He's quiet, you know? One minute it was just Erin and I in the room, and I was looking at this chair in the warehouse, then suddenly he was sitting at a desk. It surprised me."

"I see." Lex said, leaning back against the headboard, taking me with him. *I'm certain he wants me to stay awake, but leaning against him like this isn't helping.* "And Derek? How do you know him?"

"I told you—I know Erin. She's my best friend. We've known each other since kindergarten. We were inseparable until she went away for college. That's where she met Derek. She fell madly in love, got married, and then she got knocked up."

I could feel the rumble in Lex's chest as he let out a deep laugh. "That was eloquently stated."

"Thank you. I try."

"You know what I think?"

"What?" I asked, draping one arm around him as I nuzzled against his chest.

"I think you're going to be trouble."

"Probably."

"I also think it's too late to walk away."

Yawning again, I let out a soft sigh, "Probably." I could feel his chest rumble as my eyes slowly closed again. "I didn't know you were going to be there tonight."

"I wasn't planning on it, but I'm glad I was."

"You surprised me."

"I could say the same for you."

"Why?"

"Because I want to be with you," he said in a heartfelt tone. "I just can't decide if it's a bad thing or good thing."

Nuzzling his chest, I shrugged my shoulders. *I don't know if any of this is good or bad. All I know is whatever it is—I can't stop it.*

The touch of his fingers brushing my back was so calming, and I was completely lost in the comfort it brought me when I heard him say, "Don't go to sleep."

That was the last thing I remember him saying before I drifted off into a deep sleep.

Chapter Six

Stretching my arms above my head, I slowly opened my eyes. Softly touching the tender bruise on my face, I recalled the details of last night. Sitting up, I realized I was no longer in my clothes. Instead, I'm wearing and oversized long-sleeve shirt and a pair of boxers, which I know for a fact, are not mine. *The last thing I remember is Lex telling me to stay awake. When did I change my clothes?*

Oh my God! Did I sleep with him? My eyes went wide when I noticed my dress and bra hung over the chair in the corner. *I have absolutely no idea what happened last night.* My palms began to sweat and my breathing became erratic. Control is something I need to possess at all times, and right now I was spinning wildly with absolutely nothing grounding me. Pressing my palm to my head, I try to remember the details of the house. *We came in and went into a kitchen, and then he walked us down a hall and up some stairs.*

Pushing the blankets off of me, I pad across the soft carpet and followed a beautifully carved handrail down the stairs. When I hit the bottom stair I turned to the left, following the long hallway into the kitchen. I looked around for any sign of Lex, but the large kitchen was empty. Noticing a window near the table, I peered outside, but once again there was no sign of him. There was no sign of anyone. It was a large, empty, grassy field surrounded by an old wooden fence. *Where the hell is he?*

Taking a deep breath through my nose, I rolled my shoulders, trying to release the tension in my neck. Scanning the kitchen for any possible sign of Lex, I spied a sticky note stuck to the fridge.

If you find this and the coffee is still hot, it's fresh.

-Lex

Despite the many questions I now have lingering in the forefront of my mind, I carefully pressed my fingers to the glass coffeepot on the counter. Thankfully it was still hot. After searching the cabinets for a mug, I poured myself a fresh cup. Sighing, I leaned against the counter taking a sip.

"This is new."

Jumping at the sound of the deep voice, I spilled coffee down the front of my shirt and onto the floor. "Holy shit!" Turning around, I looked for something to clean myself up.

"Towels are in the drawer just to the right of the sink."

Nodding my head, I grabbed a towel and cleaned myself off before wiping up the coffee I had spilled on the floor. "I'm so sorry. I didn't realize anyone else was here."

"That's funny—neither did I."

Tossing the towel into the sink, I stood up and found myself staring at Logan. Only he wasn't standing—he was sitting in a wheelchair.

"I know what you're thinking. Is it the chair that makes me look so incredibly handsome, or is it me making the chair look so incredibly handsome? It's just a zebra question. Black with white stripes or white with black stripes. Either way, it still has stripes and I still look handsome."

"Um—" Swallowing, I tried to gather my thoughts so as not to offend him. "I'm sorry, I didn't realize—"

"Realize what, exactly?" Arching his eyebrow, I noticed the same icy look he gave me the other day. *Is he defensive? Is that why he was so cold the other day?*

"That you lived here. To be honest, I'm not quite sure where here is." Glancing around the room, I looked for Lex.

"Here is my home, that I happen to share with my idiot younger brother."

"Right. Brother?" *Lex failed to mention Logan being his brother.* "So, not just business partners then?"

"Nothing gets by you," he replied sarcastically. Logan placed a mug on the counter, eyeing the coffee pot. I filled his cup and he gave me a quick nod of his head as he took his first sip. *This feels so awkward. I barely know Lex, and now I'm wearing what I hope is his underwear, while I'm drinking coffee with his brother in the kitchen.*

"I have to ask—what happened?" Logan asked, motioning toward my face. My fingers brushed against my cheek in an automatic response. *It's still sore, but it doesn't hurt as bad as I thought it would.*

"I have foot in mouth disease. I had a flare up last night and someone decided it would be best for my medication to be served with a backhand to the face."

"Funny enough—my brother has that same disease. Was the backhand female or male?"

"Definitely male. He was quite burly."

"Wait—a guy hit you and my brother didn't knock his ass out?"

Shrugging my shoulders, I took another sip of my coffee. "I believe he attempted. I wasn't prepared to be hit like that. I mean, who's really expecting to be hit. It was a bit of a shock. I fell back and was getting up when Lex leapt over me. The next thing I knew he was on the ground with me. I wasn't having any of it, so I got up and took care of it."

Setting his coffee down on the counter, Logan folded his arms behind his head and leaned back in his chair. "You're telling me my brother got laid out?"

"I'm not sure 'laid out' is an accurate description. Either way, it doesn't matter. I didn't take self-defense classes for a year to let someone hit me. I started telling the guy off and he came at me again so I kneed him in his groin." Looking over at Logan, his eyebrows rose. I wasn't sure if he was impressed or shocked, so I continued relaying the events of the night. "Then I slammed my palm into his nose. Lex decided it was time to go and now here I am."

I have never personally witnessed a crazy person laughing before, but I'm almost certain this was close. Logan was bent over with his hands wrapped tightly around his waist laughing so hard he was gasping for air. "This is great—you're great. All of this is great." Taking a deep breath, Logan looked up at me with an impressively huge grin. His smile reached past his ears and I could almost see devil horns emerging on the top of his head. "This is fantastic."

Wanting to change the subject, I decided to introduce myself. "I'm Indie, by the way. We met the other day. I came with Erin."

"I knew I recognized you. I'm sorry if I was short with you the other day. I had a lot on my mind, and my disagreeing brother wasn't helping. I keep trying to expand, but he just wants to stay local. Not that you care about any of it."

"I understand where you're coming from on the expansion. The detail in the furniture is amazing—it's so elegant. You can tell that whomever made it, loves their work."

"I'm not sure if he loves it as it's more of a distraction for him. You can ask him for yourself—he's out in the barn. Come on."

Grabbing my coffee, I followed Logan out the screen door in the kitchen and down the ramp into the barn. Lex was shirtless once again, sanding some sort of railing as we walked in. He was completely lost in his work and didn't notice us until Logan cleared his throat a few times

"Morning, brother. Tell me, how did it feel to have a girl defend you? She says she knocked the guy out after you fell to the floor."

"Hey—that's not what I said." I threatened Logan with a glare.

Completely ignoring me, he gave me a wink before turning to face Lex again. "She's being modest. I heard he was quite a monster."

"Screw off, Logan. A real man would never hit a lady. His mother didn't teach him right, so I was going to. I tripped, and he caught me off guard. I would've knocked his ass out if Indie hadn't gotten to him first. Hell, I had to throw her over my shoulder just so she didn't kill the guy."

Logan looked over to me, raising his brow. "I'm impressed. My brother got himself a feisty one."

Brushing his hands off on his dark blue jeans, he walked over to me, wrapping one arm around my waist while looking at Logan. "Your brother is now ignoring you." Turning to face me, his fingers softly brushed against the side of my face. "Does it hurt?"

"A little. How's your lip?"

"Swollen. It's not my first fat lip—I'll live." Leaning down he pressed his lips to mine, and I fell victim to his kiss, completely forgetting that we were not alone.

"Gross. Go make out somewhere else." Logan said, making fake gagging sounds as he spun his chair around.

"You know where the door is."

Giggling, I pulled back from Lex's grasp and waved to Logan. "It was nice meeting you again."

"You too. Now get a room." The door closed behind him and I wondered for a split second which brother was the bigger smartass.

Another giggle fell from my lips as Lex pressed his lips against mine, completely ignoring his brother. "Stop laughing, you'll only encourage him."

"I think he's sweet."

"He has you fooled. Logan is not sweet. He's an idiot."

"Huh—he said the same about you."

"Did he now?" Picking me up by the waist, he set me on the long, wooden workbench in front of him. His hands gently spread my legs open as he moved to stand between them. Just the touch of his skin against mine had my heart racing.

"So—he's your brother?" I questioned.

"Yeah."

"That's a bit more than a business partner, don't you think?"

"Technically, I didn't lie."

"Acts of omission aren't any better. On another note, why am I in different clothes?"

"You asked for them—don't you remember?"

Searching my brain, I vaguely remembered waking up and complaining about my clothes being twisted. Lex was lying on the blankets beside me and tossed some clothes at me.

Covering my face, I tried to hide my embarrassment as I remembered asking him to close his eyes. "God, I'm so sorry you had to deal with any of this. He must have hit me harder than I thought."

"Are you sure you're okay?"

Looking up, I see deep blue eyes filled with genuine care for me. "Yeah, I'm fine." I found myself holding my breath as he looked at me.

Hesitantly resting his hands on my knees, Lex chewed on his bottom lip. "I just want to try something."

"Okay." Giving him permission, I leaned back, a bit curious of what he had planned. Dragging his fingers up my thighs he smashed his lips against mine. Lex's hands encircled my waist as my fingers found their way to his neck, locking him against me. His tongue swept across my bottom lip and I opened to him. He played me like a skilled musician plays their instrument. With every touch of his fingers my body sang a different note, perfectly in tune with him. Pulling his lips from mine, his fingers softly traced my skin under the collar of my shirt as his gaze swept over my body. *I have never felt this hungry for someone's touch before.*

Feeling brazen, I pulled the shirt over my head and tossed it onto the bench beside me. His hands grasped my hips, squeezing them, as his mouth traced the path his fingers just took. Wet kisses traveled down my chest to my stomach and back up again. My body hummed as his tongue found my nipple, sucking it into his mouth. *Holy shit. This isn't how I pictured my morning, but I'm not going to stop him.*

Running his fingers along the waistband of my shorts, he started to roll them down, but stopped as he lifted me off the bench. "You need protection."

Wrapping my legs around him tightly, I looked him in the eye, questioning his choice of words. "What?" *Protection from what? From him?*

Grabbing the shirt I was just wearing, Lex laid it across the bench, making sure to smooth out all the wrinkles. *Oh. That kind of protection.* He tapped my legs and I unwound myself from him. Setting me on top of the shirt, he leaned me back against the countertop with a long kiss. I was breathless when he broke the kiss and tapped my hips. My back arched as I raised them in the air. His touch scorched my skin as he rolled down my shorts, revealing the white silk panties I had on from last night.

"Those are sweet," he said with a wicked grin. Leaning down, he placed a kiss on the small bow intricately placed in the center. A gasp left my lips as his fingers slipped under the material and straight into me, making me forget where I was. My hips flexed against his hand as he stroked me, making my nerves twist into a tight ball. Just as I was about to find some relief, he pulled his fingers from me, and popped them into his mouth, licking every bit of me from his fingers.

"Holy fuck." I said breathlessly.

Laughing, he gave me a devilish grin as he pulled my panties off. "Now I want to try something else."

Oh, shit. Were we still on the 'try something' thing he mentioned? I thought we had sailed way past that.

My tongue swept out, wetting my lips, as I watched him pop the button on his dark blue jeans. Slowly pulling down his zipper, his jeans fell a bit lower on his hips, revealing his black boxer briefs.

"Open those legs." he ordered.

My legs spread farther apart upon his command. His fingers grasped my hips, pulling me closer to him, until my legs were hanging off the edge. Freeing his cock from his boxers, he stood, staring at me, while slowly stroking himself. Without breaking eye contact, he rubbed the tip of his cock up and down my slit, paying special attention to my clit. My eyes closed as he slammed into me, digging his fingers into my flesh. Pulling almost completely out, he repeated the action. This time, pressing so deeply into me that I could feel the rough hardwood under the shirt scrape against my back. *Fuck. Me.*

"Again." I begged. His hand left my waist, pulling at my breasts as he thrust back into me. My hands climbed his arms to his neck, pulling him down onto me as he continued to slam my body into the hard bench. *It's hard. It's fast. It's rough, and I fucking love it.* My eyes flew open as he twisted my nipple, pulling on it just the right way to make me sing. "Fuck."

"I know—I fucking know." His words were rough and strained. The vein in his neck bulged as his fingers dug into my body, grasping onto me. Slipping one hand between us, his fingers found my clit, circling it until my nerves explode around him. Shuddering gasps left my chest as I came undone. *This is everything I've needed—everything I've wanted, and so much more.*

"Oh shit." Closing his eyes, he pulled himself from me, spurting his release all over my stomach. "Fuck," he groaned.

"Uh huh." I mumbled.

We were both breathless as he grabbed a blue cloth from a hook on the wall above us. Wiping off my stomach he leaned down, placing the gentlest of kisses on my lips. Pulling my hands, he sat me up. Tapping my feet, I slid each leg back into my panties. His hands lifted me from the bench and stood me on the floor beside him as he grabbed the shirt I was lying on. Shaking the shirt a few times he held it over my head, and I slid my arms into the sleeves, watching in confusion as he fixed himself and pulled up his zipper. "Come on, city girl, let's get you out of this barn."

One-night stands are nothing new to me, but I felt let down by the loss of connection with him. He went from commanding alpha, back to the confusing man I met in the bar, in less than thirty seconds. *What am I doing?* This was supposed to be fun, but warnings were flashing around me as I followed him through the house and up the stairs to his bedroom.

Standing in the doorway of his room, I watched him as he rummaged around his room grabbing clean clothes. "Lex, what are we doing?" I asked.

"Right now, we are going to go shower and then I'm going to take you back. As much as I'd like to keep you, I don't think your friends would like it. Besides, a shower seems like the easiest way to get you naked again," he replied with a devious smile on his face.

"Is that your goal then—to keep me naked?"

"I just want you. Your naked ass standing, soaking wet in front of me is a bonus. Come on—we're both covered in sawdust now. We need to shower before it gets in weird places—if it hasn't already."

Looking down at my hands I noticed a dark brown stain on the side of my palm and sawdust sprinkled on my forearms. The control I like to possess slipped a little more from my fingers as I stared at the dirt on my body. He had me so distracted I didn't even notice the mess I'd let myself become.

I followed him across the hall to the bathroom, immediately noticing the deep blue walls with white trim encasing the room, making it feel smaller than it really was. It's not a color choice I would have made, but to each their own. Two towels were already lying haphazardly on the matching blue rugs. One lonely toothbrush and a rolled-up tube of toothpaste were lying on the edge of the sink. If I could choose two words to describe this room they would be *bachelor* and *pad*.

Lex turned toward me after turning on the water in the oversized glass shower in front of us. "Sorry if there's a mess. It's just me here."

"Am I the first girl you've had up here?" I asked sarcastically. I was only half joking as I bumped him with my shoulder. *I wonder when the last time the mirror above the sink held a woman's reflection?*

Lex stripped his clothes from his body, opened the shower door, and stepped underneath the steady stream of water. "The last time a girl was in this room was nine years ago," he replied.

"Oh? Who was she?" *What the hell is wrong with me?* Mentally castrating myself, I tried to save myself from more embarrassment. "I'm sorry—that's none of my business."

"You're right—it's not. Now are you going to get undressed or do you plan on taking a shower clothed?"

Sighing at my own idiocy, I stripped myself of the clothes he so graciously let me wear and stepped into the hot shower with him. "Oh my God! It's cold!" Jumping back from the water, I smashed myself against the shower wall.

"It's not cold."

"Are you insane? Is your external body thermometer broken? That water is ice cold."

Chuckling at my reaction, he spun around, adjusting the knobs until warmer water began to stream down across my feet. "Better?"

"A little. It's still too cold for me."

Turning the temp up again, he jumped toward me as the water hit his back. "Shit, that's hot."

"Thanks for the compliment." Pinching his ass, I spun us around until my back was fully immersed in the hot water cascading from the showerhead.

"There are three things you need to know," he said.

Tipping my head back under the water, I ran my hands through my long, wet locks. "Oh?"

"One, never pinch my ass again. Two, that water is not hot— it's scalding. I think some of my flesh may be peeling off." Wrapping his arm around my waist he pulled me to him.

"And three?"

Dropping his hand back to his side, his eyes turned a deep shade of blue. "The last woman in this room was my mother, and she was beyond beautiful."

"Oh." I caught on two things as he stared at me. The first was how sad his eyes became when he mentioned his mother. The second was his use of the word 'was.' *I made a joke about his deceased mother.* Feeling like the awful person I was, I adjusted the knob in the shower, cooling down the water just a bit. *I want to hold him, and I know he won't step back into the water with me until its cooler.* Tugging on his fingers, I pulled him under the stream of water with me. *There are so many questions I want to ask, but now is not the time.*

We spent the rest of the time in the shower washing one another, with subtle kisses every time our lips came close to each other. Neither of us spoke. It was the first time I had ever felt comfortable enough with a person to not use excuses or sarcasm to get myself out of a potentially awkward situation.

After our shower, I slipped my clothes from last night back on, minus the sandals. *It's going to take a lot of effort to get those back on, and right now I don't want to do anything but sit on this bed and watch him move around his room, wearing only a pair of boxer briefs.* Catching my gaze, he gave me a wink, giving his ass a little shake while bending over to pull up a pair of jeans.

"Lex, if I had singles I would be tossing them in every direction at you."

"Huh—I didn't picture you being a fan of strip joints."

"Oh, I'm not. I just like your ass."

A deep baritone laugh escaped him as he leapt toward me, tackling me, and pinning my arms above my head. "You are a smartass."

"Caught on to that, did you?"

"I like your mouth." His lips pressed against mine while his tongue demanded entrance. I opened to him and my body hummed to every move. *Jesus. This man strums every string just right.* "I need to get dressed and take you home before I end up stripping you naked again."

"Can I have option two, please?"

"Fuck me." he said with a low growl.

"That's the idea."

Shaking his head, he pushed himself off of me as he grabbed my hand, taking me with him. "Time to go, temptress."

Sighing, I relented to him. *He's stuck on taking me back to Erin's.* I got one last glance of his perfectly chiseled chest before he pulled on a dark gray t-shirt.

My time with him was up, as I followed him downstairs with my sandals and clutch tucked under my arm. Logan was downstairs, bent over a bunch of papers at the breakfast nook tucked under a window. Looking up, I gave him a wave goodbye and he gave me a noncommittal head nod as we walked out the front door.

"What's up with him?" I asked.

Lex linked his fingers with mine as he closed the door behind us. "He's trying to come up with more designs. He wants to expand and says we need to be 'edgier.'"

"I think he's wrong. The design is impeccable. Everything is so ornate and detailed. You just need to find the right buyers to expand. I wouldn't change the designs."

Placing a kiss on the top of my head, he opened the passenger door of his truck. I climbed in and put my seatbelt on. I waited until Lex shut his door before I bombarded him with questions.

"Why not just expand what you have?"

"Why not just keep it the way it is?" he retorted.

"I don't know. I mean…I would love to be able to get my hands on some pieces. If you had more warehouses or employees you could double your income—reach more people."

"No."

"But why?"

"Leave it," he replied firmly.

"Fine." Sighing, I dropped it. *It's not like any of this will have an impact on my life. It's just so beautiful, I don't understand why he wouldn't want more people to see his work.*

It didn't take long for me to notice the familiar scenery on the country back-roads. Soon we were pulling up the long brick driveway leading to Erin's front door. Putting the truck into park, Lex turned to face me. The crease in his brow had me worried for a second until he gave me a wink, followed by his perfected devilish smirk.

"Let me see your phone."

"My phone?" I questioned.

"Yeah. Unlock it for me, please." Swiping a pattern on the screen of my phone, I unlocked it and handed it over. He stared at it, confused for a second. Then, he nodded his head as his fingers started tapping on my screen. The console between us began to make a ringing sound as he handed me back my phone. "Now I have your number."

"Oh." *He could've just asked. I would have given it to him.* Taking my phone back, I dropped it into my clutch.

"Tomorrow night there's a small party a friend of mine is throwing. He throws it every year, but I haven't been in a long time—I'll pick you up at seven. You'll love it."

"Shouldn't you ask me if I want to go? Assuming makes an ass out of you and me."

"That mouth." Chuckling, he scrubbed his hand over his face. "Fine, will you go with me to a party tomorrow night?"

"Sure, pick me up at seven." I replied sarcastically. Leaning over, I planted a kiss on his cheek and hopped out of the truck. As I shut my door, I noticed the stunned look on his face. *Ha! For once I've left him speechless.*

It's only after I've walked up to the door that I realize how still it seems. I was worried about what I was about to walk into. Turning the knob in my hand, I opened the door.

The house was completely silent. Grasping my sandals and clutch to my chest, I snuck up the stairs to my tower.

Chapter

Seven

Hot water is a necessity to life, and I refused to leave this shower until I've used every drop. I tried talking to Erin several times yesterday, but she wasn't having it. Things between her and Derek must still be rocky from the other night. Neither one was speaking to the other. Non-committal grunts were passed between one another. The only person anyone seemed to be talking to only said a handful of words and wore a diaper. Olivia seemed to be loving all the extra attention. I couldn't blame her—people waiting on you hand and foot must be nice.

Wringing as much water as I could out of my hair, I wrapped a towel around my body and jumped across the hall into my bedroom. *I highly doubt anyone would climb the stairs all the way up here, but then again, it's clean so someone must be coming up here regularly.*

Pushing open the door, I jumped backwards at the sight of someone sitting on my bed, and I tripped over my towel. I ended up briefly lying naked in the hallway before grabbing my towel to cover myself back up. "Shit."

"Crap, I don't have my phone. That would have made for some great blackmail."

"Screw off, Erin. You scared the shit out of me." Making sure my towel was secure I walked back into the bedroom. "I was in the shower."

"I know."

"And yet you're in here waiting for me? Did you possibly consider the idea that I might be naked when I came back in here?"

"No, but I wish I would have. Get dressed, I can see your nips." Falling back on the bed, Erin covered her face while she laughed hysterically.

I rummaged through my clothes for a minute before sliding on a pair of black, silk panties and a pink and white polka-dot bra. I am a firm believer in not having matching underwear. It's an unrealistic goal, and one flaw that I can live with. Slipping on a pair of dark gray leggings and an over-sized, long sleeved, black tunic. Erin was now propped up on my pillows, messing with my phone.

"It's locked."

"It was worth a shot. It keeps going off, you know."

"Give it to me."

"Nope." Completely ignoring me she tucked my phone underneath a pillow. "Derek isn't mad at you," she said suddenly.

"Well he shouldn't be, and I never said he was." Grabbing a brush from my luggage, I started untangling the knotted mess that was my hair.

"I'm not mad at you either," she added.

Setting the brush down on the dresser, I climbed onto the bed next to her. "But you wouldn't talk to me. All I wanted to do was talk to you about him, and you just ignored me."

"Maybe I should clarify—I'm not mad at you *anymore*. You keep ditching me for Logan's brother. First you go to lunch with him, which was fine. I want you to have fun, but then he doesn't talk to you for four days and all you do is mope around my house. Then when I finally get you to go out, you get into a fight and he swoops in, carrying you off into the sunset."

Sighing, I laid my head on her shoulder and pulled her hand into my lap. "You're right, I did mope. I like the way I feel with him. But you're also wrong—it wasn't into the sunset. It was nighttime. He took me to his house and was the perfect gentleman—until we had crazy hot sex on his work bench."

Pulling her hand from me, she sat up gasping as she stared at me. "I knew it. You slept with him. You're such a slut."

"I am not a slut." I replied, feigning hurt.

Scoffing at my attempt to claim my innocence, she rolled her eyes. "Be serious—what happened?"

"What do you mean what happened? You want a play by play?"

"Yes. No. Wait—I don't know. Don't judge me. I'm exhausted and I haven't been laid in a month. I'm not sure I remember what it's like."

"Oh, sweetie, that's sad."

"It's not that we don't try. It's just that Olivia ends up needing me or the hospital calls. The world is against me."

"I'm sure 'the world' is cock blocking you. I bet it has a list, and every morning when the world checks it, you're at the top. It sits down for morning breakfast and pulls out the list. 'Cock block Erin. Check.'"

"Shut-up! Be serious—tell me what happened. I'm living vicariously through you."

"Well, at first he wouldn't let me sleep. He was worried because I hit my head. I remember lying with him on his bed. He was so warm." Closing my eyes, I remembered the way it felt to have my body wrapped around his. "Then this morning when I woke up, I found him in the barn. We had sex in the barn on his work bench and then we took a shower together."

"Back up—you were in a barn. Voluntarily?"

"I know—it was weird. Speaking of, how do you get stain off your hand?" Turning my hand over I showed her the faded brown stain still stuck on my skin. "We both tried washing it off in the shower, but it didn't work."

Grabbing my wrist, she spun it a couple of times. "Wow."

"I know. He took me fishing the other day and it didn't freak me out as much as I thought it would. I mean, I wasn't touching the fish he caught, but I was standing by the water in dirt while holding a fishing pole. I like it and I don't. My palms get sweaty, but when he touches me none of it matters."

Erin squealed as she bounced on my bed. I instantly put my guard up when she clapped her hands like a deranged lunatic. "This is fantastic."

"Oh no, stop. This is just me having fun, and you're not ruining it for me."

"Relationships can be fun, Indie. It happens all the time."

"That's all propaganda brought to you by Hallmark. I've witnessed what *love* can do to a person."

"Kent was an asshole. You can't compare him to Lex."

"Fine. Then explain my parents."

"What they had or have isn't normal, Indie. You need to realize that. Let go. Maybe Lex is exactly what you need to crawl out of your shell."

"No. My shell is comfortable. It's set up just the way I like it and there's only room for one person. Now, if you're not busy, start braiding my hair. He's picking me up at seven for a party."

"I knew it! This is so much more than fun. You're practically dating."

Sighing, I spun around, flipping my hair in her face. "Listen, you can either braid my hair and not mention the word relationship again, or you can leave and you won't get any more juicy details from me."

"God, you're such a bitch. Let me grab a brush." Hopping down off the bed, she grabbed a brush and hairband from my makeup bag. "Scoot closer to me, I can't reach your big, fat head with you so far away."

Smiling, I scoot closer to the edge of the bed so Erin could braid my hair. We may not see each other all the time, but our friendship hasn't changed. I'm still a bitch, but for some reason, she still tolerates me, and I love her for it.

Ten after seven. It was the third time I had checked the time on my phone in the past ten minutes. I was pacing back in forth in the living room. Poor Olivia was sitting on the floor moving her head back and forth as I walked past her. *I'm going to end up making that poor baby dizzy.* Sitting down in an armchair, I checked my phone again. *Eleven after seven.* Sighing, I relent to the idea that I may have been stood up.

"He's probably just running a few minutes late. Don't stress yourself out," Erin said, handing me a small glass of water. T aking a breath, I knocked the glass back and relished in the cold liquid pouring down my throat.

"You're right. God, what's wrong with me?"

"I'm always right. See?" she said pointing towards the window. She gave me a smug smile as I jumped up and walked to the door while Lex parked his truck.

"A lady lets the gentleman come to the door."

"Good thing I'm not a lady. Love you." Waving to Erin, I opened the door and closed it tightly behind me. Lex was already halfway to the door when he saw me. I slowly walked over to him, as he looked me over from head to toe.

"You own shoes that tie?" he asked in a surprised tone.

Looking down, I twirled one of my feet in the air, showing off my black converse. "I do. They're cute."

"I see that. You ready?" Slinking one arm around my waist he pulled me closer to him. *It doesn't matter where he takes me tonight, as long as I'm this close to him, it won't make a difference.*

"Yep." Leaning up on my toes, I placed a kiss on his cheek. He helped me into his truck and soon we were winding around the country roads. I kept hoping he may stop the truck and teach me how to dance again, but he was concentrating on the curves of the road. *I have never seen him so serious before.*

"Lex, is everything okay?" I asked in concern.

"What? Yeah, it's fine. These roads make me nervous."

"Okay. You always seem so cocky. I would never have thought you were capable of being nervous."

"These roads freak me out. My buddy lives just over the state line in Tennessee. As beautiful as you are right now, I really need to watch the road. Accidents happen when you aren't careful." he said, his voice dropping to a whisper.

Glancing over at him, I studied everything about him. *It's not just his face that's making me nervous, it's the white of his knuckles as they grip the steering wheel. He's scared—and he knows these roads.* Not wanting to make the situation worse, I sit quietly in my seat for the rest of the drive.

The sun sank lower into the sky as we drove along the winding roads. By the time Lex pulled up the dirt path and threw the truck into park, the sky was a beautiful shade of purple with just a kiss of orange on the horizon. I had never witnessed a sunset more beautiful. My eyes left the horizon as I turned to face Lex, who was still gripping the steering wheel as though his life depended upon it.

"Lex?" I cautiously asked.

"Indie." His grip loosened on the steering wheel, but just barely.

"Is this the place?" Hoping to distract him, I decided to ask more questions about the large field we had just parked in. "This is a field. Were we even on a road just now?"

"This is the back ten of my buddy's property. Those lights in the trees lead to a big pit he fills with branches and trees that fall on his property. Every year he has a bonfire in the pit. It's the official mark of summer, or at least that's what he claims. It's really just a reason to have a fire and drink some beer with friends."

"So, shoes that tied were a great decision on my part."

"Yes, shoes that tie are good. Come on—I want you to meet him." Jumping out of the truck, Lex walked around to my door and helped me step out onto the dirt path. There were a bunch of cars and trucks parked on both sides of the narrow dirt path. It looked haphazard to me, but then again, I'm not used to any of this.

Taking my hand, Lex led us under large oak trees with tiny white lights hanging from the branches. *I'm not sure how they have electricity this far away from a building, but whatever their method is, it works.* The lights twinkling around us made me feel like I was walking through stars. It was breathtakingly beautiful. At the edge of the trees was a large grassy area with a bonfire in the center. It must be at least ten feet wide and six feet high. The heat from the fire kissed my cheeks, as we got closer. I felt so drawn to it.

A heavier set bald man wearing a red t-shirt with a half-naked woman on it walked up to Lex and smacked him on the back. "Holy shit! I cannot believe what I'm seeing. Fucking Alexander Clark. You finally left your fucking house. Somebody beer me. This fucker is getting drunk tonight."

My eyes flashed toward Lex as the man almost knocked me over. Clearing his throat, Lex tightened his hold on my hand and pulled me closer to him. "Brett, I'm not drinking tonight. I won't drive on those roads like that."

"I hear ya, man, I do. Just one beer though. It won't hurt ya'."

"I said no. Also, you're rude as hell."

"How's that?"

"Your fat ass almost knocked over my girl." Lex wrapped his arms around my waist, before picking me up and setting me in front of him. His thumbs made soft circles on my hips and I melted into his body.

"Fuck me runnin'. You gotta' girl?" Brett let out a deep laugh before taking my hand. "Enchante. It's a pleasure to make your acquaintance, madam," he said as a ridiculous, fake French accent rolled off his tongue.

"Um—hi?" Not sure what to say to him, I pulled my hand away and grabbed onto Lex's forearm.

Leaning down, Lex rested his head on my shoulder. "The idiot you see in front of you, who thinks he's impressing you, is also known as Brett. This is his place."

"Oh." *No wonder this guy seems overly friendly.*

"Brett, this is Indie."

"Indie? Like the race?"

"Actually, it's Indigo. My friends call me Indie for short."

"Well, it's a beautiful name. Grab yourselves a chair. There's beer in the cooler."

Brett nodded toward the fire as he walked away to greet someone else.

"He was right, you know." Goosebumps prickled my skin as Lex's words brushed across my neck.

"Who was?"

"Brett. Your name is beautiful, just like you."

"Aww. That's sweet. You do know pick-up lines aren't necessary anymore? You already have me."

"No, but they're fun. Besides, that wasn't a pick-up line. It was a compliment."

Leaving one arm wrapped around my waist, Lex led us closer to the fire, where worn wooden benches and chairs were set up, curving around the pit. Coolers were strategically placed between every few seats, while small clusters of people were gathered around a few coolers. Others stood close to the fire, talking and laughing with one another.

The sky faded into a midnight blue as we sat beside one another, staring at the fire. He only left me a few times to refill our drinks. His fingers circled the skin of my wrist as he sat back down beside me, handing me my drink. It almost looked as though someone threw glitter into the sky and it scattered as far as the eye could see. The way the stars twinkled so tightly in their clusters made it almost impossible for me to spot the constellations. It's like the universe was built around this starlit sky.

"They're almost as beautiful as you."

"What?" Looking up, I saw Lex staring at me with a soft smile playing on his lips.

"The stars—they are almost as beautiful as you."

"That's the nicest thing anyone has ever said to me."

"It's true." His fingers brushed against my cheek. Grasping my chin, he pulled my lips towards his. Just as I began to lose myself in the moment I heard an obnoxious voice screaming over the music and people talking around us.

Lex sighed, dropping his hands into his lap. "Fucking Janet."

"Who?" Turning toward the yelling, I recognized the skinny brunette from the bar. She was yelling at Brett, poking him in the chest with her finger. He wasn't having any of her attitude, and he pushed her away, yelling for her to leave. She spun around and tripped, catching herself on a chair. When she gained her footing, she looked up and saw us staring at her.

Her eyes narrowed as she stepped toward us. *Fuck. She must recognize me from the bar. I don't want her spoiling this night for us.* Pulling on Lex's arm, I motioned for us to go, but it was too late. She was already screaming, but it wasn't at me. She was screaming at Lex.

"You shouldn't be here," she shouted.

Looking up at her, Lex squeezed my hand. "And you're drunk. Go home."

"It's your fault I'm like this. You did this to me." she accused.

"Janet, stop. I didn't put that drink in your hand."

Laughing, she tilted her head back, slamming the rest of her drink, but not before spilling a little on her dark blue shirt. "Oh no, you didn't give me anything. You just took it all away. That's what you fucking do."

Irritated with the way Lex was just letting her berate him in front of everyone else, I stood and placed myself between them. "Listen, I don't know who you are, but it's obvious you're drunk. Just fuck off. He doesn't want to talk to you. I'm not sure anyone here does. So just go crawl back into whatever hole you came out of."

"I know you! You're that bitch that threw shit at me."

"Nope—wasn't me. I've never seen you before in my life. Just go." Laughing, I crossed my arms over my chest. She could barely stand as she wobbled on her feet. Thankfully, the burly man that stood up for her the other night was nowhere to be found. I had no problem knocking her on her ass, but I'm not sure I needed to make that kind of impression in front of Lex's friends.

She stepped to the side, sending daggers straight toward Lex. "Is this your girlfriend, Lex? No—oh no—you don't deserve love after everything you did." Licking her lips, she swiped her hand through her curls, pushing them back out of her face. "You stupid girl." She was still looking at Lex, but I guess she was talking to me. "I wouldn't go around defending a murderer."

A gasp left my lips from the sting of her accusation. *What the fuck is she talking about?* Turning toward Lex, I could see his head fall as he looked toward the ground.

"See? He won't even deny it. Go on ask him. The only thing he's good for is killing the ones he loves. Just ask him." Her black, hatred filled eyes finally met mine. *I've had enough. Lex is sitting with his head in his hands and I will not let her break him like this.*

Spinning around, I raised my arm, but she was already gone. Brett was dragging her away. Tossing her to the ground, he yelled at her as she crawled away, "Stay the fuck out! You're not welcome here."

Giving me a nod of his head, he turned the music back up and everyone went back to what they were doing. It was as though they didn't just watch their friend break in front of them. *Some friends they are.* Kneeling on the grass in front of Lex, I gently placed my hands on his arms.

"Lex, whatever she said, I don't care. She's drunk. None of it matters."

Shaking his head, he looked up at me with a tear rolling down his cheek. "She was right."

"What?" I asked in confusion.

"She was telling the truth. I always hurt those I love. Just ask Logan. I t's my fault he's in that damn chair."

"As much as I want to delve into whatever you're trying to tell me, I think we should go. She's obviously psychotic and you're obviously not in the condition to be able to handle her." Lex stared up at me as I held my hand out. *I'm not backing down from this.* "Lex, if we don't go, I'm going to go find her. Will you be able to stop me? You couldn't stop me last time."

Shaking his head, he put his hand in mine. I led him away from the fire and his so-called friends. He stopped by a tree a few feet away from his truck and began to dry-heave. *He didn't have anything to drink. What could be causing this?* I wondered. Pressing his hands against the trunk of the tree, he held himself up. If I didn't know better, I would have guessed he had too much to drink, but he hadn't touched a drop.

"Lex—"

"I feel like I'm going to be sick."

"I see that. Give me your keys, I'll drive us back."

"You don't know the roads."

"Lex, you're bent over in front of a tree, ready to puke at any given second. Some drunk lady just accosted you in front of all your friends. You are not in the right state to drive. Give me your keys. You can tell me which turns to make."

Shaking his head back and forth he pushed himself off the tree. Placing my hand on my hip I challenged him with an arched brow. I wasn't backing down. Relenting, he pulled his keys from his pocket and handed them over to me. "Indie, please drive slow. Promise me we will go slow."

"Slow. I promise. If it makes you feel better, I'll put the caution lights on and go as slow as you like until we get back to your place."

Staring at me with fear laced in his eyes, he walked around me and hopped into the passenger side of the truck. *I guess we are in agreement then.* I slid into the driver's side and adjusted my seat. Lex was so much taller than me; I was practically on top of the steering wheel before I could reach the pedals. Putting the key into the ignition, I started the truck and pulled back onto the dirt path leading to the main road.

The yellow caution lights flashed eerily against the trees, brush, and rocky edges of the road as we drove. I wouldn't go over twenty miles per hour. We were barely inching along on the road, but I wasn't used to these curves, and every time I'd try to speed up, Lex would look like he might get sick.

Chapter Eight

By the time we reached his house, all of the color had faded from his face. I put the truck into park and handed him back his keys. When I started to open my door, he stopped me.

"She was right."

"Are we doing this now?" I asked.

Looking down at his hands, he shook his head back and forth. I hopped out of the truck and walked around, opening his door for him. He didn't say a word as he grabbed my hand in his and led me into the house. His palms were clammy and damp to the touch. *Whoever that bitch was, she has completely ruined him. It appears Janet and I are going to have a talk, whether she likes it or not.*

Logan was washing dishes when we walked into the house. He gave me a questioning look and I shrugged my shoulders in response. *I have so many questions to ask them.* Lex shook his head, as if to say no to us, and led me up the stairs.

Pushing open his bedroom door, he immediately took off his shirt. Noticing the wet marks on his shirt, I realized his hands weren't the only thing sweating. His breaths were becoming quicker as he paced in front of his bed with a confused glaze in his eyes. It suddenly hit me, *He's having a panic attack.*

I rushed into the bathroom and wet a hand towel he had lying by the sink. Folding it up as best as I could, I ran back into the bedroom and placed it on the back of his neck. He jumped at first, but he relaxed some as I led him to the bed, pushing on his shoulder for him to sit. Deep blue eyes stared up at me as I ran my fingers through his hair. *This needs to pass on its own.* Nothing I could say would help him, so I stood in front of him, holding the washcloth for him. Taking deep breaths, he leaned his head against my stomach and ran his fingers up and down my thighs. Eventually his breathing slowed back to normal and his hands wrapped around my waist, pulling me closer to him.

"Thank you," he said sincerely.

"You're welcome. If it helps, I get those too."

Nodding his head, he let out a sigh against my stomach. "I ruined our date."

"No, whoever that bitch was, ruined our date. I'd like to get my hands on her. Who the fuck does she think she is accosting you like that in front of all your friends? Repulsive bitch."

"The repulsive bitch, as you so eloquently put it, is Logan's ex-wife."

Pulling the washcloth from his neck, I took a seat next to him on the bed. "What?" I asked in confusion.

Lex scooted up against the headboard and pat the bed, "Indie, come here."

Scooting next to him, I laid my head on his chest as he stroked his fingers up and down my back. "Why would she say that about you?"

"Because it's true. This isn't the easiest thing for me to talk about. Fuck, I don't think I've ever talked to anyone about it, to be honest. Everyone kind of just knew what happened. Logan has tried a couple of times, but I brushed him off. I know what I did, and seeing him in that wheelchair every day is a reminder of my poor choices."

"I don't want you to do anything you don't want to do. If you need me to forget any of this happened, that's okay."

Sighing, his fingers stopped, pausing in the middle of my back. "You're the first person who hasn't judged me, but I guess that's about to change. Logan was always the mechanic in the family. If it had a motor, he could fix it. When I was in high school he was working at a local garage and started bringing tools home to help me fix up a beater I bought off one of the neighbors. Fast forward a couple years. I was going to school in California on a scholarship for baseball. I was a phenomenal catcher. Nothing got by me. I was so good my agent called—I had been picked up by a league."

"Wow. You're that good? But you make furniture." My fingers slowly traced his fingers that were now wrapped around me as he held me against him.

"Was. In my excitement, I got cocky. I used all the money I had saved up over the years and had a guy in California finish the work on my car so I could drive it back when I came to tell my parents the news. I guess it was my way of showing off how I had escaped this town. I was on my way out, and they were so proud of me." His breath hitched a bit as the tone in his voice dropped. Pausing my fingers, I leaned up on my elbow, watching him wipe a tear away.

"Lex—"

"I'm fine—it's fine. Anyways, on what was supposed to be the last day of my trip, I took them for a ride in my car. It was sleek as fuck. Deep, plum purple paint. Chrome rims. It was a mechanics wet dream."

"What kind of car was it?"

"A 1969 Dodge Charger. She was my baby. I got everyone packed in the car and I started showing off. She handled the road like a pro. Despite the rain we had the night before, I was pushing her hard around the curves. My mom was getting nervous, yelling at me to slow down, but my dad and Logan were in the back, screaming with excitement. I ignored my mom and started taking the curves a little faster. The back tires would spin a bit on the wet pavement, but I kept going. As we got closer to my buddy's place I noticed a few semi-trucks passing us. They were really kicking up water with their tires. It was a warning—and I didn't take it." Another tear rolled down his face as he turned to look out the window.

I didn't know what to say, so I lay back down on his chest, wrapping my arm tightly around his waist. Gently placing a kiss on his chest, I waited for him to continue.

"I lost control of my car and slid down a small ravine. We must've flipped a couple of times because we ended up hanging upside down with the front of my car stuck on a tree."

"Jesus." I didn't know what else to say. It was painful just to listen to him talk about it, so I couldn't imagine living it.

"I remember looking over at my mom. She was pinned to the seat with part of the tree in her chest. She never had a chance. My dad started talking to me and I wanted to get him out, but he made me help my brother first. So that's what I did. It took me a bit to get Logan out. His legs were stuck and I couldn't open his door. Finally, I broke the window and pulled him out. Once I got him off to the side I ran around the car to my dad, but I couldn't open his door. I remember an insane amount of heat coming off the car. I pulled and pulled, but I couldn't do it. Then everything flashed. I woke up in a hospital a few days later with two dead parents and a brother who would never walk again."

Of all the things he could have told me, I would never have guessed any of this. I was stunned. He survived an almost impossible situation and saved his brother in the process. He didn't see what I saw. I saw a man who admitted his mistake, and almost gave his life to save his family. It didn't matter how any of them got in that situation, what mattered was that he tried his best to save them. What I didn't understand was how she fit into this. "And Janet?"

"Fuck her! None of us liked her to begin with, but my idiot brother was obsessed with her. She convinced him she was pregnant and they got married right after their high school graduation. She lost the baby a few weeks later, but she wouldn't let Logan go to any of her appointments or anything. She was weird about it. We often wondered if she made it up to trap him."

"That's awful. Who does something like that?"

"Fucking trash. They fought a lot and she liked to hang around with other men while my brother worked during the day. He found out and started questioning her, but she swore up and down it wasn't what he thought. Then, after the accident, when she found out the odds of him being able to walk again, she started sleeping around again. Except that time, she didn't even try to hide it. She would bring the men home to their apartment. One day, I was bringing Logan back after a physical therapy appointment and we caught her in bed with two other guys. He kicked her out and filed for divorce the next day."

"That's fucked up."

Sighing, Lex brushed his hands up and down my back. "That's not even the most fucked up part."

"There's more? What else could she possibly do? Holy shit, someone needs to write this down and sell this shit as a reality TV show."

Chuckling, Lex kissed the top of my head. "There's always more when it comes to Janet. She tried to sue my brother for slander and defamation of character after their divorce because of the rumors going around town. The judge threw the case out when she stood up and yelled at Logan, calling him a worthless paralyzed fuck. Then she started yelling about how she could never be with someone who couldn't provide for her the way she needed. The last straw was when she said she didn't want her future children to have a disabled father, and she wished he would've died in the crash because then she would've been able to collect on his insurance policy."

"Wow. That's just—I don't even know what to say to that. Wow."

"I know. She's a bitch. She's been ruining our lives ever since. Blaming me for ruining her life isn't new. She started drinking heavily after that, and even though I hated her, I knew it was my fault. She got pulled over a couple of times and they finally hit her with a DUI. She was required to go to meetings and since I was the reason she was drinking, I figured the least I could do was drive her. The meetings didn't last though. I'm so afraid she's going to kill someone because of me, so we have an unspoken agreement. She gets trashed, I drive her home."

"After everything she did, you still help her?"

"Janet, the way she is, and Logan, the way he is—that's all on me. My parents not being here. All of it. It's all on me."

"And Logan? What does he say about this?"

"He doesn't know."

Brushing his hand from my shoulder, I sat up and I looked down at the broken man beside me. There were no more tears, but the pain was still evident in his eyes. "When's the last time you talked to someone about this?"

"I already told you—I haven't. Everyone already knows."

Nodding my head, I chewed on my bottom lip, carefully choosing my next words. "They know the timeline of events, but do they know what happened to you?" His brow furrowed as he stared back at me. "The accident happened—I can't imagine the guilt you been carrying. What happened to you wasn't just the car accident. You saved your brother's life, while at the same time, losing your parents, all while dealing with your own injuries. To make matters worse, your brother's wife turned psychotic and blamed her addictions on you."

Not understanding where I was going with this he just stared at me with a confused look on his face. "Thank you for summarizing my guilt for me. That was so helpful."

"Just listen to me for a second. You gave up California, didn't you? The baseball—did you go back to it?"

"No. I stayed here. Logan needed me."

"And you've stayed here ever since, taking care of him and dealing with the judgment from everyone else. You're not a murderer, Lex. It was a car accident. You said it yourself...the trucks were kicking up water. Do you know for a fact if you would have slowed down that you could've prevented the accident?"

"No, but it might have helped."

Shrugging my shoulders, I repeated his words back to him. "It *might* have helped. You don't know that for sure. You have been paying penance for something you couldn't have prevented. I see that look in your eyes...you don't know for sure what would've happened. How long ago was that?"

"Nine years ago."

"Nine years? You've been hurting and holding onto this for nine years? Jesus."

Linking his fingers with mine, he gently brushed my knuckles. "Are you going to leave? It's getting late."

"It's been late. Why would I leave?"

"Because I ruin everything I love. I touch things and they shatter."

"I'm not going anywhere, but I need you to make me a promise. Janet is a cancer. The guilt she is putting on you is metastasizing. She's a poison—walk away from her. Don't run to her when she calls. You are not responsible for her."

"You don't understand—"

I interrupted him, "No, I do understand."

"You don't know how it feels to know you are responsible for ruining lives. I love my brother, but look what I've done to him."

Sighing, I gave up on trying to get him to see it from my point of view. *I'm not sure anyone will ever be able to help him carry that guilt.* Slipping off my shoes, I laid back down on the bed beside him. "Lex?"

"Yeah?"

"Love is overrated. All it brings is pain and shattered pieces. I've witness it destroy families and marriages. Don't put so much faith in it. It's a hallmark fascination brought to you by an armed fable character with a bow and arrow."

Kissing the top of my head, he squeezed me against him. "I'm too tired to touch on that tonight. Can we put a pin in that and delve into your hatred of Cupid another day?"

"Sure."

I'm not sure how long I lay there, staring out the window at the stars, but it was long enough for me to realize that whatever this was between us—it was more than just lust. *Fuck Cupid if he thinks he can control me. I can't fall in love—I won't. Nothing good ever comes from it.*

Chapter

Nine

The skin on my neck prickled as something brushed across it. I tried to wave it away, but it happens again. A deep hum vibrated against my skin, while something rough grazed against my flesh. Fingers gripped my waist causing my eyes to flutter open, only to close again when Lex's lips find my skin. A soft moan fell from my lips as his mouth finds my ear, lightly nipping it with his teeth.

"Morning," he whispered.

Arching my back, I push my ass back against him. *Now I have an itch that needs to be scratched.* "Morning."

"I want to thank you for last night," he said, as his hands softly slid under my shirt, making small circles with his fingers on my skin.

"I'm not sure I did anything worthy of a thank you."

"Trust me, you did." His lips found the curve of my neck, sending goosebumps racing across my skin.

Reaching behind me, I pulled his body closer to mine. Feeling something hard pressed against my ass, my body instinctively ground back against it. Grabbing my hips, Lex rolled onto his back, taking me with him. Flipping myself around, my legs straddled his hips as our lips met, delving into a sea of knots. His touch was electric, waking every nerve I have.

"Naked—fuck. You need to be naked." At some point during the night, he was smart enough to take off his pants. I, on the other hand, wasn't. Lex's hands began pulling at my shirt. Raising my arms above my head, he pulled it off and tossed it to the floor. Unclasping my bra, I tossed it onto the pile of accumulating clothes, as his rough hands palmed my breasts, pulling and twisting my nipples. *Fuck.* He continued to pull at the remaining clothing, frustrated he couldn't touch me.

"You want me naked?" I asked sarcastically.

"Yes, I fucking want you naked. I'm going to die by hard-on if I'm not inside you soon."

Laughing, I unwound myself from him and slipped off my leggings, taking my panties with them. Standing beside him in all my naked glory, his fingers traced up the inner part of my thigh. Brushing his thumb against my clit, he slipped his fingers inside of me. My eyes met his as I grabbed onto his forearm, securing the fate of my orgasm before he could pull away. His dark gaze scorches me, making me crash around him as his fingers expertly worked my clit.

"Oh, shit." Short, breathy gasps exited my lips as he hooked his fingers into me, using them to pull me closer to him.

"I need that wet pussy."

Grinning with hazed eyes, I climbed back onto the bed, straddling him, with his cock positioned under me. I hovered for a second before slamming down onto him. I don't know who was more surprised by the sudden rush of movements, him or me, but we both let out a 'fuck' as I raised my hips to do it again. I intentionally tried to slow my pace, stretching out my lingering orgasm, but he wasn't having any of it.

Yelping as he flipped us over, tossing me onto the mattress, his hands parted my thighs as he lifted my hips and slid a pillow underneath them. Using his thumbs, he spread my pussy apart before running his tongue straight up the middle.

"Oh." I moaned.

A smirk played at the corner of his mouth as he caught my gaze. He does it again, but this time, he sucked my clit into his mouth while swirling his tongue around in a circle. *Holy. Fuck.* His lips worked their way up my body, softly kissing me as they went until they find mine. Our tongues clashed. The taste of sex filled my senses as he thrust into me, catching me completely off guard. With my hips tilted, he went so much deeper than our first time on the workbench.

His fingers gripped my skin, digging into me. "Fuck. I'm going to come."

"Oh God. Please." I begged.

"What?" he asked in shocked concern as he stilled inside me, cutting off my impending orgasm.

"I'm on birth control. Fuck, I want you to come. I want you to let go." I quickly explained.

His deep blue eyes stared down at me for just a second before picking up his relentless pace. His thrusts became harder, more desperate—until finally, I came undone. I was in a haze of orgasmic bliss when I heard him groan, losing himself inside of me. *I've never let a guy do that before. Hell, I've never wanted anyone to do that, but watching him lose control knowing I'm the reason is the sexiest thing I have ever witnessed.*

His head dropped to my chest, pressing soft kisses against my flesh while his arms clung to me. "Never—never in my life." he said breathlessly. In that moment I knew he was feeling the same exact thing as me.

"Fuck." The current between us was heavy, thick, and electric. Rolling onto his side he curled his leg over me, cocooning me with his sweaty body. My head pressed against his damp chest as he tucked me under his chin. My whole body was damp with sweat. *I'm a mess and in desperate need of shower. Either he's fucked me to the point I know longer care about personal hygiene, or I've let my guard down long enough to let him in.*

My stomach sank at the thought of the pain this was going to cause me later. It was at that precise moment, I decided to let go of enough control to lose myself, and I clung to him as he held me against him. *Cupid be damned.*

The soft kisses being placed on my neck spread across my shoulder, and I was completely undone as I lost myself to him once again.

"Just how long do you plan on hogging that bed?" Lex asked.

Sighing, I opened my eyes to see Lex standing at the foot of the bed, fully dressed. I crumpled my nose at the sight. "It's comfy," I whined. Pushing out my bottom lip, I give him a little pout. "It would be even better if you were in here with me."

"And as tempting as that sounds, you've broken me, lady. Twice in one morning is all you're going to get from me. Come on––I want to show you something," he said, tossing my pants and one of his shirts at me. Realizing he wasn't going to give up, I kicked the covers off me and started pulling on my leggings. By the time I was finished getting ready for the day, Lex was already downstairs waiting for me.

"There she is. I was wondering if I had to come back up there. You were taking an awful long time."

Shooting Lex an annoyed glance, I took the coffee cup from his hand. Slowly sipping the heavenly drink, I eased myself down onto a barstool.

"Afternoon, sex freaks." Logan said teasingly.

Great. Now I know Logan either heard us or he's making assumptions. Either way, that was not something I was expecting to hear while waking up over my morning cup of coffee—even if it was late afternoon. Coffee flew from my lips as I spit my drink out, choking on what was left in my throat. Lex handed me a towel and softly rubbed my back.

"Remember when you said you thought he was sweet?" he asked sarcastically.

Wiping off my face, I tossed the towel onto the counter, cleaning up my mess. "Yeah, I retract my statement. You were right—idiot stands."

"Ouch. You two have wounded me with your sharp words. I'll have you know, I'm a genius." Logan said, dramatically clutching his chest.

Arching my brow, I mentally question his description of genius. When I looked up at Lex, he just shrugged his shoulders. "Technically, he's not wrong. He took a bunch of tests and people in white lab-coats certified it."

Logan grinned at me from his wheelchair as he rocked his feet up into the air. I was still trying to process how genius equaled a brother making sex jokes in the kitchen, when Logan leaned too far back and started to fall. Lex and I both gasped, jumping to catch his wheelchair. To my complete surprise, Logan corrected his chair, laughing hysterically. *Fucker*. My heart was pounding in my chest, all the while he was playing us like the fools that we were.

"Fuck you, Logan. That was not funny." I shouted.

"Aww, don't get mad at me, Indie. It's not my fault you were outsmarted by a certified genius."

"Evil genius, maybe, but you're still an idiot."

"Thank you." Lifting a glass of orange juice off the counter he held it into the air to toast to my words. "Whenever you two get done screwing like jack rabbits, you'll find me in the office. I'm working on some new drawings. Lex, all joking aside, I think you'll like these this time."

Nodding his head, Lex took a sip of his coffee. I was still angry from shock when Logan began humming while wheeling himself out of the kitchen. He even did a fancy spin before leaving through the door. Rolling my eyes, I turned to Lex who was smirking, while reveling in the notion that he was right. "He is an idiot." I confirmed.

"I told you so."

"How long have you been waiting to say that?"

"Since the day you walked into the bar. It's been killing me. You have no idea what a relief it is. Weight has been lifted off my chest. I feel so victorious."

"You know, Lex, sometimes sarcasm can be classified as a narcissistic trait."

"Get used to it. I speak fluent sarcasm. Besides, doesn't being a narcissist mean I think of myself as a God?"

Sighing, I poured myself some more coffee. "But, Lex—you're not a God."

"That hurts, Indie. That really hurts."

"You're too late. Logan already won the Oscar for best drama today."

"If I didn't know any better, I would think you're crabby when you wake up."

Shrugging my shoulders, I finished my coffee. Carefully placing my mug in the sink, I spun around to face Lex who was still leaning against the counter. His shirt was tight around his shoulders, causing the memory of last night and this morning to creep into my mind. *He's definitely a God, but I'm not telling him that. If anything, his ego needs a little deflating.*

"What did you want to show me?"

"Come with me, city girl. You'll love this."

Grabbing my hand, Lex led me from the kitchen, outside to the barn. He started pulling tarps off furniture he had stacked along the sides of the barn, muttering to himself about not being able to find something, while I was completely lost in the exquisite furniture. The details of the carvings in the wood were so precise. *None of this has been machine made.* You could tell by the subtle curves and deep expression. *This was made by hand. I wonder how many hours it took him to perfect these.*

"Found it!"

"Found what?" As I looked over at Lex across the barn, I fell speechless. Underneath a worn, dusty tarp was a beautiful full-length mirror. Eccentric, clawed feet stood proudly at the base with what looked like a lion's tail curving around one of the legs and up the side of the mirror.

As I approached the mirror I could see the detail the artist put into it. *This isn't a modern piece. This is much older.* The curves were smooth, but had tiny peaks to them, markings left behind from a chisel or a small planing tool. My fingers ran along the dark mahogany edges.

"My grandfather made this as a wedding present for my grandma. It sat in my mom's room for a long time. Sweaters, belts, and pants would be draped over the top. It was dusty—I never thought she used it." A soft smile took over his features before it faded just as quickly as it came. "Logan and I were playing baseball in the house and my dad told us to take it outside, but neither of us listened. I was standing in the hallway and Logan ran into my parents' room. We were pretending there was a runner on third and the goal was to tag him out." Rubbing his hand on the back of his neck, he walked around the mirror, stopping beside me.

"What did you do?"

"Third base was the mirror, " he said reluctantly.

Closing my eyes, I shook my head. "Of course it was a base. What is wrong with you? Why on Earth would you choose this as a base?"

"I don't know—I was a kid. It seemed like a good idea at the time. Anyway, I threw the ball as hard as I could to Logan, but he missed. Instead of it landing in his glove, the ball shattered the glass."

"Oh my God! I bet you caught some serious shit for that. My mother would have killed me, or sent me away to a boarding school just for touching it, let alone breaking it."

Lex laughed as he wrapped his arms around my waist, pulling my body against his. I liked the way my body fit to his when he rested his chin on the top of my head. "My mom didn't kill me, but she wouldn't talk to me for a few days. That was the worst punishment she could've ever given me. I knew I had disappointed her, so I promised to fix the mirror for her. Of course, I didn't know how, but I wasn't going to let that stop me."

"I'm assuming you fixed it?"

"Yeah." A deep sigh left his chest, resonating through my body. "I always pushed it off. Every year I promised I would get to it. Life is funny that way. It's the small things you didn't notice that mean the most. After my mom died, I hid from everything. Then one day I found the mirror. It didn't take me long to fix it, but then I started fixing other things my dad had left in the barn."

Spinning myself around in his arms, I wrapped my hands around his neck and pulled his lips to mine. "But you did fix it. Maybe you just needed more time."

"Maybe. It doesn't matter anymore."

"One mirror started all of this?" I asked, motioning around the room.

His eyes glanced around the barn, pausing at the mirror. "I guess so."

"Well, that's one hell of a mirror." Out of the corner of my eye, I spied a rocking chair propped up on his workbench, next to some sort of stand. *Maybe I can steer us away from this heavy moment.* "What's this?" I asked as I walked over to the bench, running my hands along the rungs of the chair before pointing to the stand.

"The hospital is having a fundraiser for a children's charity. Logan and I always donate a piece to be auctioned."

"That explains the chair, but what's this?"

"Oh, that's a stand of sorts that I'm working on. I was hoping they could use it in the play center at the hospital. Kind of like a television cart, but for game consoles." Walking toward me he pointed to the different sections. "See? The shelves roll out. This way, the kids can reach the game consoles and games better. Plus, I put hooks under the shelves so the cords won't get tangled. Oh— and check this out, I put Velcro straps under the shelves too. Now they can store the controllers without wrapping them up with the cords or losing them." Bending down, Lex showed me the straps and hooks. He even included a shelf on the side of the stand that was made to hold cups so they wouldn't spill. The stand still had the carved feet, but carefully turning it over, he showed me the hidden wheels.

"I've never seen someone so excited about a television stand before."

"It's more of a game center, but call it what you want."

"Game center works perfectly. Are you always this excited when you build things?"

"Sometimes. I get this excited when I'm around you. Maybe it's contagious."

"Oh no—I wouldn't want to infect you. Maybe you should stay away."

Laughing, he stood and pressed another kiss to my lips. "Not a chance, city girl." Lex led me around, showing me other pieces he had finished, before leading me from the barn back into the house.

We spent the rest of the afternoon under the covers in his bedroom, talking. I could feel myself letting go a little more each time we were together—it was terrifying.

It was after seven when I finally asked him to take me back to Erin's. He was reluctant, but he did it anyway. After we arrived, we sat in his truck for a few moments longer with his lips attached to mine. I didn't want to let go so I poured everything into that moment with him.

Stepping out of the truck, I softly waved as I watched his headlights fade into the distance. When I entered the house it was quiet. Deciding to go to bed, I slowly climbed the stairs to my ivory tower. With each step I took, I could feel myself shattering a little more. My anxiety was beginning to get the best of me.

What am I doing? I'm so afraid of being hurt...or used again. This is why I'm better off alone. I mentally chastised myself as I ascended into my tower in the sky.

Chapter

Ten

The summer seemed to quickly be slipping through my fingers. I had been in Alabama for a couple of weeks now and most of my time had been spent with Lex. He makes me feel so beautiful and in control of everything, when in reality, I'm not. I hadn't spent more than a couple of hours looking for a job or a place of my own. Even though I sold my business for a decent amount, I can't live off of it forever. Eventually, I will need something permanent to anchor me to the ground.

Staring at the cursor flashing on my laptop, there were two apartments pulled up on the screen. Both were beautiful and spacious. One was a townhome, not too far from the river, with an amazing view. The other was a house for rent, which is settled on two acres, between two other vacant lots. The land is overgrown with weeds and wildflowers, yet it still looked beautiful to me. I'm leaning toward the house, but I haven't made my final decision yet. I have to let the rental company know which one I will be choosing by tomorrow morning.

Erin suggested asking Lex what he thought, but I can't do that. At first, I was going to tell him when I started looking for a place, but I couldn't find the right way to bring it up. Since I don't have to decide until tomorrow morning on which place I want, I decided to put off telling him for one more night.

Closing my laptop, I started getting ready for my date with Lex later. He wouldn't tell me where we were going. *I just hope it's something fun and exciting.* There's a pit in my stomach, as though I were standing on the edge of something, waiting to fall. It's not that I'm scared or put off by it—it's quite the opposite. For the first time in a long time, I was excited for whatever life brought next.

"Are you going out again tonight?" Erin asked, twirling her hair around her finger as she leaned against the doorframe to my room. My eyes caught her gaze in the mirror as I perfected my lip-gloss. "It's just that you've been here over a month, and I've only seen you, maybe a handful of times."

"We just went to breakfast yesterday. Then after that we took Olivia shopping. I wish you would have let me get her that hat. It looked adorable on her."

"No. That hat was neon green. No one should wear a hat that bright. Don't dodge my question either. I get that you like him, I just wish I saw you a little more."

Sighing, I set down my makeup and turned around to face my best friend. "You're right, I'm sorry. Do you want me to cancel?"

"Nope, but could you repeat that one more time? I'm not sure I will ever hear those words fall from your lips again."

"Do you want me to cancel?" I asked. Smirking I gave her a little wink. *I know what she's after.*

"Nope. Try that again. Say the first part. The part before you asked if I wanted you to cancel." Arching my brow, I shook my head in the negative. *There's no way I'm saying it.* Erin tugs at the bottom of her shirt, sticking out her bottom lip just enough to make me feel guilty. *She's evil. There's definitely something wicked about her.*

"Fine. I'll say it again—you're right."

"Yes! I got it." Erin flashed me a smile as she held up her cell phone. "I recorded it. There's no way you can ever deny it now."

"That's low, Erin, even for you."

"True, but it is what it is. Now if you'll excuse me, I need to go wait downstairs for Lex to get here so I can show him my proof.

"You are ridiculous."

"Yep, but you love me."

"I do. Can you explain why, because I don't really understand it right now?"

"I'm letting you stay in my house rent free until you find a place. That puts me on saint level. I'm untouchable. That's just one of the many reasons why you love me."

"It's just a few more days. I think I'm going to sign on the house rental."

"Good. Your use of water is going to make the river run dry. I'm not going to take the blame for it, so it's better if you have your own place."

"Shut up! You're so dramatic."

"Just another reason why you love me." Giving me a slight wink, she closed my door behind her, leaving me to finish getting ready for my date.

Walking down the stairs, I could hear Lex's voice. *I'm not sure what Derek and him are talking about, but I'm glad they are finally talking.* When I got downstairs, Erin was sitting on the couch with Olivia at her feet. Every time Erin would get the blocks stacked up to resemble some sort of house or castle, Olivia would knock them over by kicking out her feet. Both cracked up as the blocks tumbled down onto the floor. I still couldn't picture me ever having children of my own, but I could see the draw. Olivia looked at Erin as though she held the world in the palm of her hands. I couldn't help but wonder for a brief second if I ever saw my mom that way. Then again, I'm pretty sure you need a soul to be able to love someone. That was something I don't think she has ever possessed.

"There's my girl." Lex said, smiling as I stepped into the kitchen. He was leaning against the counter with a beer casually propped up in his hand, resting on the edge."

"I don't belong to you," I quipped. Grabbing a mug from the cabinet, I poured myself a fresh cup of coffee.

Rolling his eyes, he reached his hand out for me. "I don't think you'll ever belong to anyone. You're too stubborn."

"I like to call it independent."

"Fine. You're independent. Now can I touch you? You may be independent, but I'm not. I need you." Lex's hand snaked around my waist as I stepped closer to him. The pull my body had to him was magnetic. Wherever he was, I felt drawn to him. Gravitational pull, magnets, or maybe it's just where I'm supposed to be. *Whatever it is...I like it.* My heart rate quickened with each inch that disappeared between us. My tongue darted out, wetting my lips, when suddenly the sound of Derek's voice reminded me that we weren't alone.

"So, what are you two love birds up to today?" Derek asked.

Lex looked down at me with bright blue eyes and I know that whatever he has planned will be perfect. "Nothing too exciting, I thought we'd go for a swim in the river."

This isn't perfect at all. My eyes went wide as I pictured dirty water, seaweed, and god knows what else lurking in the water, ready to attack me. "Are you fucking insane?" I shouted. "That's not happening. Not now—not ever. Do I look like a person who wants a bacterial infection or fish nipping at the skin on my toes?"

Derek's laugh echoed around the room as Lex pulled me closer to him. "I told you she wouldn't go for it." Lex said with a laugh.

"You were right. I'll tell ya, Indie, I've never witnessed someone freak out about a river before. Where do you think the water in your coffee comes from?"

Spinning in Lex's arms, I turned around, crossing my arms over my chest as I glared at Derek. "Obviously from an organic, filtered rain cloud hovering in the sky. It's called filtration, Derek. The water in my coffee doesn't have fish shit in it."

"Well, not that you know of." he replied in a sarcastic tone.

Eyeing my coffee, I shrugged my shoulders as I took a sip. *That's one risk I'm willing to take.* Lex's deep baritone laugh vibrated through my body as I leaned against him with his arms still tightly wrapped around my waist.

"Where are you really taking me tonight?" I asked in concern.

"I thought we'd all go out for drinks. What do you think?" A smile spread across my face. *This is perfect. Now I can spend time with Lex and I'm not casting Erin to the side.*

"Yes! This is great! Erin, we are going out. Get your ass ready!" I shouted in excitement. Spinning quickly in his arms, I pressed a kiss to his lips, while at the same time spilling some of my coffee on the floor.

"One, don't scream like that unless you're dying. Two, you better clean that up. I just mopped." Erin snapped.

"Fine, but you're not killing my buzz. We are going out. Call Clarissa or do whatever you need to do. I want to go dancing." Grabbing a towel off the counter, I cleaned up my mess while Erin called the babysitter. *This summer has been unreal.* Glancing over my shoulder, I stared at the man making it happen. I had been denying it for a while, but at that moment I knew I was falling in love with him. Closing my eyes, I sent a silent prayer up toward the heavens. *Please, don't let him hurt me. I can't handle getting my heart broken again.*

Erin took her time getting ready, since we had to wait on the sitter to show up. Derek hadn't said much, so I wasn't sure if he liked the idea of all of us going out to the bar, since the last time Erin and I ended up in a fight.

Lex laced his fingers in mine, leading me into the living room where Olivia was still playing on the floor with the blocks. We built a few towers and relished in her giggles as she knocked them down while we waited.

By the time Clarissa arrived it was well after seven o'clock. In about an hour or so the sun will set and the night will officially begin. Erin fawned over Olivia for a ridiculous amount of time before Derek finally pulled her from the room and out the front door.

She was still blowing kisses as he helped her into the car and shut her door. *If they ever decide to have another baby, Erin will never leave the house. It would take her way too long to say goodbye.* Shaking my head at the scene she was making, I hopped into Lex's truck, ready for a night out.

One drink easily turned into four as Erin and I danced on the wooden floor in front of the live band. Spinning around I glance over my shoulder toward the guys. They haven't left the table. Instead, they just kept mumbling to one another and shaking their heads at us. Erin grabbed my hand and pulled me from the dance floor as she shoved her glass in the air. Glancing down at the drink in my hand, I realized it was almost gone.

"Boys, my boys, we are hot and sweaty. We needs the drinks." Erin said, pointing to her cup as though they wouldn't understand the point of her slurred words.

"No, baby, you need water. You both need water." Derek took her cup, set it on the table and handed her a bottle of water.

"Boo. You're no fun. Just help me okay. I need the pink drink in here." Erin pointed to the empty glass now sitting on the table. *I may be buzzed, but there's no way I'm as drunk as her.*

"Erin, babe, let's sit for a second. My feet hurt." I softly pushed Erin backward toward a barstool. Once it hit the back of her legs she sat down with a very loud sigh. *She can be mad at me all she wants, she's wasted, and water is probably the best idea for her right now.* Plopping down on the stool next to her, I passed my now empty cup to Lex.

"Please?" I tried batting my eyelashes for extra effect, but I was greeted with the same response Erin got.

Lex handed me my own bottle. "Water." Scrunching my nose up, I opened the bottle and relished the cold liquid pouring down my throat. The water was delicious. Alabama summers are fierce, with no forgiveness, so it was ridiculously hot, even indoors.

"Dance with me." My fingers tiptoed across the small round table, landing on Lex's forearm.

"Finish your water and then I'll dance with you."

"Promise?" I asked. A bead of sweat rolled down Lex's throat catching my attention, completely changing the atmosphere of my question.

"Promise." Lex replied, his eyes flashing a dark blue. *I hope that's a hint at what might be in store for me later.* Tilting my head back, I gulped every last drop of water.

"There—it's empty. Now dance with me." Lex took the empty bottle from my hand and gently placed it on the table in front of us. Standing, he pushed back his stool as he grabbed my hand and led me toward the dance floor.

The rhythm around us was fast and chaotic, but Lex set our pace. My back was toward his front as he gripped my waist, pulling my body close to his. The zipper on his jeans pressed against my ass, while his hands wrapped around my waist, slowly sliding up my stomach. Leaning my head back, his lips found the flesh behind my ear. Hot kisses were followed by soft nips on my neck as we slowly swayed to the music. *Fuck. Me.*

Chills spread across my skin as he spun me away from him and back again. We were completely off beat, but it didn't matter. I was locked in a deep blue gaze, lost to the man pulling my strings. I was his personal puppet as we danced. Every tug or pull of his touch had me under his spell. When the song ended, I found myself wrapped in his arms with my lips pressed firmly against his. Breaking our kiss, he lifted me from the dance floor and carried me back to the table with my legs wrapped around his waist.

"Stay." he ordered. Nodding my head, I watched as he fixed himself before heading toward the bar.

"Holy shit, Indie." Erin said as Lex walked away.

Turning toward Erin, I propped my arm up on the table. "What?"

"Is it always like that between you two?"

"What do you mean?" I asked, confusion painting my face.

"Besides the fact that you two were basically fucking on the dance floor? I'm talking about the way he looks at you. It's like he's starving and you're the first sight of food he's seen in days. Sweetie, he's going to devour you."

"God, I hope so."

I noticed Lex checking his phone while he was standing at the bar. It must not have been important because he slid it back into his back pocket before grabbing the two bottles of water from the bartender. I swallowed as he got closer, his tan boots and dark jeans stopping directly in front of me. Looking up, I was met with the same dark blue gaze, full of promises. *After that dance, I really hope he lives up to it.* Shifting on the stool, I tried to alleviate the building pressure between my thighs, but it failed miserably. *The only thing that's going to fix this is him.*

"Drink." *Fuck. Me. He's gone alpha male on me. God, he's sexy when he's like this.* Taking the bottle of water from his hands, I slowly swallowed the water, making sure to tilt my head back just enough to make a display out of myself. *If he wants to watch me swallow something, then I will.* I thought playfully.

"Finished." I said, handing him the bottle. He slowly set it down on the table. Grasping my face, he gently tilted my lips towards his.

"I need to be inside you. Can we go now?" he whispered seductively in my ear.

"God, yes." His lips crashed against mine before nipping at my bottom lip and dragging it through his teeth. Standing from my chair, I leaned over Erin's shoulder.

"I'm going."

Swallowing another sip of water, Erin looked over at me. "Did he say he needed to be inside you or am I that drunk?"

"Yeah, sweets, you're drunk, but he did say it and I'm going to hold him to it. I'll see you sometime tomorrow. Be nice to Derek."

"Night. Have fun. Have lots and lots of fun."

Laughing, I linked my hand with Lex's. "I'm ready."

"Good, cause I'm going to fucking die if we don't leave soon." Shaking my head, I followed him as he led us through the bar and out the front door. My feet barely touched the gravel before he lifted me into the air, tossing me over his shoulder.

"Isn't this taking the caveman act a little too far?" I yelped when his hand landed across my ass.

"You have no idea how bad I want to fuck you. If I didn't think other people would be looking, I'd take you in the back of my truck right now."

That would be so incredibly hot. "Do it." I challenged.

"What?" he asked in shock.

"Fuck me—right here."

"No way! This is all mine, and I'm not sharing with some asshole that may decide to watch us. No, Indie. This. Is. Mine." Each word was accentuated as he laced his hand around my neck. His lips crashed down upon me, smothering me in hot, wet kisses as he set me down in the passenger seat of his truck. He quickly shut my door before hopping into the driver's seat. Slamming on the gas, we were soon squealing out onto the road. He was in such a hurry, I'm not even sure he checked his mirrors.

His hand reached for mine and I noticed his knuckles were white against the steering wheel again. "I'm sorry, but I need to calm down so I can focus. Once we get back home, I'll make up for it." Not wanting to ruin the moment, I gave his hand a simple squeeze. His words and demeanor may have changed since we got in the truck, but the electric current making my heart race was still there.

The beams from his headlights shone across the front porch of his house. The truck was barely in park before he jumped out and opened my door. "Legs." he ordered. Confused by what he meant, I started to step out when he lifted me from the truck. Instinctively, I wrapped my legs around his waist. "Legs—I need to feel you on me."

"Fuck, 'on you'—I want you inside me."

"I'm trying. Fuck, I'm trying." Kicking open the front door, Lex threw his keys on the counter before taking us up the stairs, two at a time. My head fell back, screams laced with laughter. I was flying through the air before I even realized what was happening. Landing softly on the mattress, I started pulling at my clothes when he stopped me.

"Uh uh, that's my job." Leaning back on my elbows, I crossed my legs in front of me, watching as he slowly stripped down to nothing. Seeing his thighs flex as he stepped towards me had me squeezing my legs together a little tighter. Lex is fit and tone, but he's lean with broad shoulders and thighs that could easily support both of our weight. *He's built like a tree and I absolutely plan on climbing him.* Putting my hands up, I stopped him before he could get any closer.

"Stop."

Cocking his head to the side in confusion, he stared at me, as I slowly pulled my tank top over my head, revealing my black lace bra. My fingers moved carefully as they released the hooks on my bra one by one. Lex swallowed so loudly, I could hear it. Smirking, I reached for the button of my shorts, but he wasn't having it. He quickly grabbed my ankles, pulling my body to the edge of his bed.

"You can be in charge outside of this room, but in here, I make the rules."

"I'm not one to be told what to do."

"Don't lie—you like what I do to you." His fingers popped the button of my shorts before gripping the sides, yanking them off my body in one quick swoop. A yelp left my lips as he leaned down, using his teeth to scrape along the skin just above my matching panties. His head moved farther south, kissing and nipping at my skin as he slid them off my legs. Gripping my ankles, he pushed my knees toward my chest, spreading them apart as he stepped in between them.

I felt open and exposed as his eyes ran the length of my body. I've never been overly self-conscious about my body. I'm active enough that I've always been thin. However, the way he was looking at me was making me feel so incredibly sexy. I had no doubt I had his full attention. Biting my lip, I reached toward him, pulling him down upon me. Our tongues mixed in a fiery heat of lust. The buildup alone had me teetering on the edge of possible explosion.

He ran two fingers up my slit, pausing just below my clit. I wiggled, trying to get him to relieve the pressure I could no longer handle, but to no avail. His gaze caught mine and I instantly froze my movements. That's when I felt it. The push and pull of impending, glorious doom as his thumb pressed against my clit. Sliding his fingers inside me, he carefully curled them up just enough to make me moan. "God, I love it when you squirm beneath me."

"Lex, please." I begged.

"What? Tell me what you need."

"You—inside me. Please."

"Grab those pillows behind you," he ordered.

Not hesitating, I reached above my head and grabbed the pillows lying behind me. Without saying a word, Lex lowered my legs to the floor as he helped me to stand. He centered my body in front of him, slowly spinning me to face the mattress. Taking the pillows from my hands, he stacked them on the bed in front of me.

"Lex?" I questioned.

"Trust me. Get on the bed and kneel in front of the pillows." Doing exactly as he said, I positioned myself on the bed. His hands slowly slid up my thighs, gently pulling my legs apart. "Spread them a bit more."

Taking a deep breath, I spread my legs farther apart as his hands slowly pressed against my back until I was leaning over the pillows, with the side of my face lying against the mattress. I was bent like a triangle with pillows stacked beneath my pelvis. *This is new,* I thought to myself.

Suddenly, the tip of his cock pressed against my ass, causing me to jerk away from him. "No way!" I shouted.

"Not tonight, but eventually I will have your ass." A hiss escaped his lips as I felt his hard cock slowly slide into me. "God damn."

He slowly pulled away before pushing into me, completely filling me. The angle of my body allowed him to go deeper than he had ever been before. Another moan left my body as he quickened the pace. Lex gripped onto my hips, holding me up as he slammed into me over and over again. His fingers pinched my skin as he tightened his hold. My back was damp with sweat, my fingers were twisting in the sheets, and I had lost myself to him. My body was perfectly in tune with his.

"I'm going to come, are you ready?" he groaned.

"Fuck yes." I felt him thrust into me two more times before pulling from me, leaving me in shock from the loss of his touch. Flipping me over, he let go, releasing himself all over my breasts and stomach. I watched his eyes roll back as he bit his lip, hissing while he stroked himself. Shivers spread down my spine, at the knowledge that I was the reason he was lost in complete bliss.

"Indie, you can never leave. Never. That was fucking incredible."

"So you're going to hold me hostage in your bed?"

"After that, I'm not letting you go anywhere. You can stay right here. Then I can have you whenever I want."

Laughing, I shook my head as he handed me a towel. His eyes darkened as I slowly wiped off my chest. I was hoping for another round, but I was surprised when he crawled up the mattress, pulling me against his chest. Draping one arm around my waist, he curled one of his long legs around me, cocooning me in a blanket of Lex. *I'm sweaty, sticky, and a full-on mess right now.* The part that registered not only in my mind, but also in my heart, was that I didn't care. I was perfectly content in his arms.

Lex nuzzled against my neck before softly whispering, "Stay."

"I'm not going anywhere." My eyes slowly closed as I drifted off to sleep in the arms of the man who had broken down the doors of my heart.

Chapter Eleven

Goosebumps prickled on my flesh, and shivers spread down my spine. Opening my eyes, I reached for the covers. *I'm freezing.* Realizing that I was alone, I slipped on one of his t-shirts and headed downstairs to find the blanket I was missing. I could hear someone moving around in the kitchen as my toes hit the last step.

"Lex?" *No answer.* Slowly peeking into the kitchen, I peered around the corner of the cabinets to find Logan pouring himself something to drink. "Logan?"

"Not who you were expecting, am I right?" His voice was low and somber.

"I was looking for Lex."

"You won't find him here. He thinks he is doing the world a justice, but in reality he's just a gullible dumbass. Try not to get mad at him over this. He's changed since he's been with you."

"If you could stop talking like I know what you are talking about, that would be great. Where is he?" I asked in confusion.

"My guess is he's driving my alcoholic ex-wife home from the bar. Don't be too hard on him." Logan nodded toward the window as Lex pulled up in his truck. Not wanting to have this kind of conversation in front of Logan, I headed back up the stairs. I was trying to convince my brain that this wasn't a big deal, but at the same time my heart felt cheated.

Suddenly, Lex's voice traveled up the stairs. I knew he was talking to Logan, but I didn't want to hear what he had to say. I was too pissed to handle any of this logically. My feet were barely tucked back into the blanket when the bedroom door swung open, revealing a very worn looking Lex.

"I can explain."

"You don't need to. Logan told me where you were. What I can't understand, is why you are choosing to hurt yourself like this, over and over again. You promised you wouldn't go to her anymore."

Sighing, Lex paced around the end of the bed. I watched him run his hands over his face contemplating what to say to me next. The longer he took, the angrier he got. It was obvious to me, no matter where he was, or the situation he was in, he would choose her and it killed me. It shouldn't, but it did. *I'm being selfish and a complete bitch, but I can't help it. I handle stress well, but the sudden urge to run slowly seeps into my mind.*

"Don't look at me like that."

"Don't tell me how to look, Lex. Where the fuck do you get off thinking you get any say in how I feel right now. Part of me understands, but the other part wants to know why you chose a drunk over me? I thought we had something. I stupidly fell in love with you, and when I finally accepted the idea, you leave me in the middle of the night for a drunk slut." It took a second for me to realize the honesty of my words. Lex was standing completely still, staring at me as though I had committed some atrocious crime.

"I thought love wasn't real for you? Cupid was just a fabled character. Are you telling me he's real now?" His loud words smacked against my skin. *I never wanted to fall in love. Life doesn't always listen or go according to plan. It doesn't take what I want into consideration, it just moves along of its own accord. Now I'm left open and exposed, and he throws my words back at me?*

"You don't get to be angry with me. I wasn't the one who left to save some drunk slut. You could have woken me up and talked to me about it. You could have just ignored the phone call. There were a million other things you could have done. Why didn't you choose one of them? Why did you have to choose the one that hurt me?"

An angry tear sliced my cheek, leaving a stinging reminder of what love really feels like.

"You're wrong. I didn't choose one to hurt you. I chose to go help someone who needed me. Someone who needed to be saved."

"You want redemption—is that it? You think running to her aid is going to erase your past? That's not how it works."

Lex started pacing again, shaking his head back and forth. "You just don't understand."

"Then help me understand." I pleaded. "I can't stand back and watch you torture yourself anymore." Hugging a pillow to my chest, I curled my feet underneath me. *I'm sitting in a room with the man who I love and I have never felt so alone.*

"How can you love me knowing what I did—what I'm capable of doing?"

"You're not your past. It was an accident."

"Don't tell me what it was. I lived it—not you." Lex slammed his fist against the wall, the loud sound echoing around me. "It's not my fault you fell in love with me. What happened to a summer of fun?" His eyes fell, defeated, as he stared out the window in front of him. *He won't even look at me.*

It's not that he ran to Janet that bothers me the most. It's the fact he doesn't see how poisonous she is. All I want to do is show him how good things could be, but instead he throws my love for him back in my face. It's returned unwanted and unneeded. My heart sank deep into my chest, drowning in the pain of that realization. It hit me at that moment, *I will never be able to make him see what I see . I can't change him no more than he can change me. This is so much more than I can handle.*

"Take me home." My words were soft and hesitant, in hopes he would argue. My heart was hanging on a thin strand of hope, clinging to the chance he may challenge me, but he didn't. Nodding his head, he grabbed his keys off the dresser and walked out of the room.

Stripping myself of his shirt, I slipped my clothes back on from the night before and grabbed my clutch. With each step I took down the stairs, it became harder and harder to hold my tears back. By the time I slipped into the passenger seat of his truck hot, angry tears sliced my cheeks one after another. Not one sound fell from my lips as he drove me home. The silence between us was deafening.

The truck slowly came to a stop. Blinking, another tear fell from my watery eyes. Without giving him a chance to say anything, I opened my door and softly closed it behind me. It took everything in me not to run. I wanted to put as much distance as I could between us. He didn't pull away until I was inside, with the front door closed, completely shutting off my view of him. *Love hurts. It's nothing but a web of lies, deceit, and pain. I know this, so why do I always get myself caught in it?*

Exhaustion began to eat at me. The endless number of stairs to my room solidified my decision to head into the kitchen. The sweat on my neck began to build, as my breaths became shorter. Trying to calm my impending panic attack, I made precise, calculated moves. I grabbed a mug from the cabinet and inserted a coffee pod into the coffee maker. The lights slowly turned blue, letting me know it was ready. With the press of a button, coffee poured into my cup. *Deep breath in. Deep breath out.* It didn't stop the pain in my chest, but it reminded me to breathe.

Walking over to the sliding glass doors, I slid to the floor, making myself comfortable, as I leaned against the cool glass. When I was in New York I would lean against the windows, watching the people below me, in an effort to distract myself long enough to avoid a panic attack. My life isn't crazy, I've never been harmed, but everyone handles stress differently. The problem with me is that I don't handle it at all. I run from it, and when it catches up with me it knocks me to the ground, taking my breath away.

I missed the solitude of my apartment. Everything was in its place. Everything stayed the same. My routine never faltered. Here, there are baby toys scattered everywhere and dishes piled in the sink. It was just a reminder of what I didn't have. It's not that I want this kind of life, but with Lex I thought maybe one day I might be okay with all of this…but he didn't. *Being wrong has never hurt so much.*

I'm not sure how long I sat on the floor, though it was long enough that the tingling sensation in my thighs began spreading to my feet. *If I don't get up soon, I'll be stuck on the floor until Erin or Derek come down the stairs to find me crying on their kitchen floor.*

Not wanting to be seen as some crazed lunatic, I put my mug in the sink and headed upstairs to my tower, where a warm, soft bed was waiting for me.

Chapter

Twelve

It had been a week since I last saw Lex. He hadn't called or texted. I tried a few times, but I was never able to hit send. I just couldn't go through with it. Erin finally took my phone away, after listening to me rant for over an hour outside on the porch swing on whether I should send it or not. She snatched it from my hand and tossed it to Derek who put it on a very high shelf inside the kitchen.

I elbowed her for it, which according to her, was a little too hard. She tried to push me off the swing, but I wouldn't budge. Erin ended up falling, and flopping on the ground like a fish out of water. Derek and I both cracked up laughing until we caught the death glare from Erin. None of us have brought it up since.

Pushing my feet against the dirt, I leaned back in the wooden swing Erin fell from a few days ago. Staring up at the sky, I searched for clouds. When I was little, I always wished I could control the rain. T here was always something about a rainy day that made my tears feel more real—almost validated. It's like the world was experiencing my pain. Today, however, was not rainy. The world was against me. Today, the sun was shining brightly in the sky, birds were chirping, and I was watching Olivia play in the backyard.

"Not that I don't enjoy your company, which I do, but are you going to leave in the morning without talking to him?" Erin asked as she plopped down beside me, completely invading my space, while sipping on the straw in her glass of lemonade.

Sighing, I leaned against her shoulder. "Why is being an adult so hard?"

"Oh, sweetie, this isn't as hard as you think. It's just a little bump. Now childbirth, that's hard."

Sitting up, I rolled my eyes at her comparison. "You know, when you say things like that, it only cements my belief in not having children."

Shrugging her shoulders, she took another sip of her lemonade. "I can't help you if you're not going to tell me what happened.

You've been sulking for a week and all I've gotten out of you was that it was what you needed. It's a bullshit excuse and you know it. Why did you run?"

"I didn't run. I walked away."

"Call it whatever the fuck you want, but you're not nineteen anymore. You can't run away from the problem."

Sighing, I gave in. "Fine, if you must know, he left me in the middle of the night to pick up a drunk whore, who also happens to be Logan's ex-wife."

"Shut up! Are you serious? I had no clue Logan was even married."

"Yeah. Remember how I told you about Lex's accident? She was married to Logan at the time, but she divorced him right after. She's a vial creature. She makes my mom look good."

"Holy shit! No one can be that evil."

"You have no idea. She's a drunk—a total waste of space. In fact, you met her that night I got into a fight at the bar."

"I'm not following."

"The woman you hit with a napkin...the one that started all that shit—that's Janet. That's Logan's ex-wife."

Erin stared at me, blinking, with her mouth hanging open, completely in shock. "That's a lot to take in. I get Logan's involvement, but why was Lex picking her up? Did Logan ask her to?

"Quite the opposite. Logan can't stand her, and he hates that Lex runs to her."

"I can see that. Did you ask Lex why?"

"He feels guilty. He blames himself for the accident, for Logan, and for Janet's drinking problem…he carries it all on his shoulders."

Erin turned to me, slapping my shoulder. "You are so fucking stupid."

"What the hell? How am I stupid?"

"He didn't leave you for Janet. He left because of the guilt."

"I know. All I wanted to do was show him how to let it all go. I told him I loved him."

"And?"

"And he said it wasn't his fault that I fell in love with him. That's all he said—that's all he needed to say."

"I think you two just need to calm down. Eventually, you'll need to deal with all of it."

"Give me one good reason why I should. I could just fall off the map and I would never have to deal with him again."

"True, but what about in here?" Erin asked, tapping my chest with her finger. "He's in there and you can't run from that. It will follow you wherever you go. I'm not saying you need to make it work between you, but you at least need to say goodbye—call it closure."

Damn it. I hate it when she's right. "Thanks, mother."

"You're welcome, and quit calling me that. Your mother is a cold, heartless bitch, hopefully suffering from an STD. Don't compare me to her."

"Sorry, you're better than her."

"Damn straight. Now get your ass off my swing. You're blocking my sun with your massive shadow."

"What the hell, Erin. I was here first."

"Doesn't matter. It's my swing."

"Gah, you're such a bitch."

"You taught me well."

Giving her a soft bump with my shoulder, I walked over to Olivia and sat beside her in the grass. Watching her play and laugh at the ants crawling on the blades of grass beside her, I lost myself to my surroundings. I was lacing dandelions into a crown shape for her when Derek walked outside.

"Hey, Indie, there's someone here for you. I told him you weren't here, but he's refusing to leave. I didn't know what to do, so he's in your room."

Gently placing the crown on Olivia's head, I kissed her chubby cheeks. She squealed and ripped off the crown, tossing it on the ground beside her. Laughing, I walked back toward Erin, before heading into the house. "Erin, she's a diva. She must get that from you."

"It's definitely from her." Derek said chuckling, as Erin glared at him.

"Derek!" Erin shouted, feigning shock.

"Oh, come on, she didn't get it from me. You can't be mad at me for that too."

Shaking my head, I left the lovebirds to bicker outside about who was at fault. *Relationships are overrated.* I ascended the stairs to the third floor where Lex was waiting for me. *Why on Earth would anyone ever have this many stairs in their house?*

When my feet hit the doorway to the room, I found Lex leaning against the window, staring outside. My heart was frantically pounding in my chest, and my stomach was sinking like an elevator crashing to the bottom floor of a twelve-story building. *There are no wires or cables to catch me. This fall is going to hurt.*

"She didn't like the flowers?"

"What?" I asked in confusion.

"Olivia—I was watching you with her. She threw the flowers."

"Oh, yeah, she's a diva. I blame Erin. Look, Lex—"

"No—" Rubbing the back of his neck, he turned around, cutting me off midsentence. His eyes were a deep, intense blue. Words that I had prepared while walking up the steps faded around me, and I had nothing left to say.

He stepped toward me, wrapping his arms around my waist and pulled me towards him. Our lips met, and lightening crashed around us. This time, I broke the kiss. *I can't do this.* Placing my hands gently on his chest, I said, "Lex, I'm leaving tomorrow." A half-truth fell from my lips.

"You think I don't know that already?" Lex spun around, pointing to the small stack of boxes I had in the corner. "I can't stop you from leaving, but you can't stop me from saying goodbye."

"What do you want from me? You weren't supposed to happen."

"And yet you fell in love with me anyway."

"I did. You made the point of letting me know it was against my better judgment." Casting my eyes downward, I took a step back to allow space between us.

"For nine fucking years, I have been haunted in my dreams, and then I run into you at the bar. Do you know what happened that night when I closed my eyes, Indie?"

"No, Lex—I don't know." Moving myself even farther away him, I leaned against the dresser, gripping onto the edge. It was taking everything in me not to run back into his arms, so I pushed myself farther away.

"Not one nightmare came that night, and I haven't had one since. Instead, there was you."

"Don't say things like that."

"And, why not? Because you're scared of what that might mean? Or are you scared of me?"

"Both—okay. It's fucking both. You don't know how hard it was to walk away, and you being here isn't making it any easier."

"Then don't go. Stay."

My voice trembled as my arms wrapped around my waist. *I feel sick. This is awful.* "And what? I'm supposed to give up everything for some guy I've known for two months? I can't be with someone who doesn't love me back." I answered honestly.

Lex stepped toward me, but I held him at bay with my arm stretched out in front of me. *If he touches me I will lose this battle.* Stepping back in defeat, he bent his arms behind his head, pacing in front of me. Pleading, he said, "Tell me what to do. I don't know how any of this works. I just know I haven't felt this good in a long time. I've told you things I haven't told anyone. Fuck, I haven't even told my brother."

"And that's my fault? I didn't ask for any of this."

"Neither did I, but now that I have you...I have this...I can't go back to not feeling anything."

"You made a point of letting me know I was the only one with feelings. You don't get to change your mind when it suits you."

"Indie, please—that's not what is happening here."

"No, that's exactly what is happening. You can't love me when it's convenient. You had your say and now I'm having mine. You weren't supposed to happen. This wasn't in my plan."

"So that's it then? It's not in your plan so it just won't work?"

I could see the hurt in his eyes and I knew I'd put it there. *This needs to be over.* "Lex, just go."

"God damn it, Indigo, don't push me away. Don't kick me out. Don't turn your back on us."

Walking over to the bedroom door, I grasped the handle in my hand, as I held it open for him. "I'm not. There would have to be an us for me to do that. You made it perfectly clear that there wasn't when you chose her over me. Anything I thought I felt for you was wrong. This," I said motioning between the two of us, "Was all wrong."

"Just hear me out," he pleaded.

"No, I'm going back to New York." *Lies.* "This thing between us will never work. I can't love someone who chooses his past over me. You're broken and I can't fix you. You need someone who needs you. Someone who needs to be swept off their feet and saved from some horrible monstrosity. I'm not that girl. You can't save me—and I can't save you from yourself." The lies stung as they fell from my lips. By the way he recoiled from me, I knew they'd stung him too. Heaviness filled the air as he walked quietly out the door and down the steps without another word. He never even looked back.

Closing the door, I dropped to my knees, letting my own personal rain cloud emanate around me. *Fuck Cupid. Fuck feeling like this. I just want to fall into a deep abyss.* Once I was able to push myself off the floor, I took a long, hot shower, letting the water wash over me, taking all of my stress with it. *It was just a couple of months. I can move past this.*

Erin and Derek were both in the kitchen by the time I made it back downstairs. Both looked at me as though I might break. Ignoring them, I made myself a cup of coffee and sat next to Olivia, the only person in the room who wasn't judging my every move.

Erin's eyes followed my every move. She sighed twice before breaking the silence in the air. "Okay, I'm just going to ask. You okay?"

"Yeah, I'm fine. I went ahead and packed everything. I wanted to make sure I didn't forget anything. Movers will be at the house in the morning." I replied, doing my best to change the subject. However, I knew Erin wouldn't let me.

"That's good. And Lex?"

"Erin, for once, just let it go. Okay?"

"Fine. I'll let it go, but only because you asked me to. It's not because I think you're making the right decision. It's also not because I think you are making the worst decision in your life, but because you asked me to. I wouldn't want you to put your life on hold for something that may or may not work out, but then again, I wouldn't want you to give up on a 'what if.' Especially, if you felt something real with him, because you and I both know how hard that is for you. But don't worry, I'm going to let it go, just like you asked me to."

Taking a big gulp of my coffee, I eyed Erin over the rim of my mug. "Gee, thanks so much for letting it go and not pushing the issue."

"You're welcome."

"I was being sarcastic."

"And so was I. What time are you leaving tomorrow?"

"Movers will be there tomorrow morning, around eight. I was thinking if I was there a little early I could start with what I already have."

Nodding her head, Erin sipped on her coffee while wiping off Olivia's face. The rest of the afternoon was filled with board games and coffee, until Derek started winning at Monopoly. Once he had control of Boardwalk and Park Place, I knew there was no way I was going to come out on top. Somehow his stack of money kept increasing while ours seemed to stay the same. Erin accused him of cheating and I ended up walking away from the game. It got way too serious for a simple board game.

I was lying in bed, staring at the ceiling, going over my mental checklist. A sudden knock on the door caught my attention. Sitting up, I wiped the tears away that I wasn't aware I had until right then. Quickly running my hands through my hair, I fixed my shirt. *I'm not trying to impress anyone, I just don't want to give them a reason to pry.* "Yeah?"

Erin slowly pushed the door open. Leaning against the doorframe, she looked over at me. As usual, her eyes read me like a book. She's the only person that truly knows me and knows what it takes for me to lose control of everything. "Indie—"

I cut her off. "Don't. I won't end up like them."

"So that's what this is about then? It's not that you could be happy, it's that you're afraid you won't be."

Shrugging my shoulders, I scooted over, making room for her on the bed. "We just met. It was just nice to let go." I answered honestly.

"Then enjoy it for what it is. You were able to let go for a bit. Maybe you can learn to let go more often. Remember when we were fifteen, and we sprayed flowers onto Heather Caplan's brand-new mustang with silly string? She was pissed."

Laughing, I recalled Heather completely losing her shit in the school parking lot. We had decorated her car early in the morning. By the time school was over, it had sat outside in the sun all day. The silly string had dried, cementing itself to the paint. She eventually got it all off, but for a few days she had to drive around town with penis shaped flowers on her car.

"It wasn't my fault. How was I supposed to know that it would dry that fast? Besides, I do remember her stealing your boyfriend at the time. If my memory serves me correctly, you caught them under the bleachers. And didn't he blame you for not putting out enough? Wasn't that his excuse? Plus, that bitch went along with it."

"You're right, but I still don't think writing 'cunt-canoe' on her car, and decorating it with penises was the best way to get back at her."

"It was perfect, and I still claim all rights to that word. Besides, they were penis shaped flowers. It's not like I decorated it with a bunch of random dicks. They were classy dicks—in a floral art-form."

"No one is arguing the awesomeness of that word. I'm not even going to touch base on your penis argument. My point was how happy and carefree you were. You've always been one that saw what you wanted and took it. You never held back on anything then. Now—you're locking yourself away. It's just that you have lost focus. Where's the Indie I used to know?"

Leaning against her, I pulled her hand into my lap. Answering honestly, I said, "I don't know."

"Promise me something—when you get settled in your new place, promise me that you will find her."

"I'll try." I answered.

"I will take that as a, 'Yes, Erin, I will do exactly what you say because you know better than me.'"

"I wouldn't go that far, but yeah, I'll try."

"One more thing, while you're still listening to me. You're not your family. Alcohol, cheating, drugs…it's not you. It never has been. Love is messy, and it may hurt, but it's totally worth it."

"Can we just pretend for a minute that we came in here to talk about something other than me?"

"Sure. Olivia pooped out a crayon this morning…at least I think it was crayon. It was a teal-ish blue color with a purple swirl in it. You know, I'm not sure what that was." Erin said, getting sidetracked. "Crap! Derek!" Erin yelled, leaving me sitting on the bed with a horrified look of knowing way too much about her kids' poop. *This mom thing has taken her down roads I'm not sure I'm willing to go.*

Messing with a few more things, I finally gave up for the night. *Anything I don't have ready now, I can easily do in the morning. Tomorrow I'm going to start over. No more distractions. No more postponing my life. It's time to focus on myself.*

Chapter Thirteen

Trying my best to ignore the pudgy man in the ugliest blue-jean blazer I have ever laid my eyes upon, I turned toward Erin, whispering over my shoulder, "If this realtor circles around me one more time, he is going to get punched in the throat. I realize this is the seventh building I've looked at this month, but I want it to be perfect."

"Stop it. You're just being picky. Stan is doing his best."

"I'm questioning your judgment in people right now."

"He's good at his job. He was able to help us find our house, and even helped negotiate the price down ten thousand dollars. Trust me, he's good."

My eyes followed the round man in front of us, as we talked about him in hushed whispers. His black trousers were clashing with his jacket, and it was seriously bothering me. When he called me yesterday about a new warehouse he found, I wasn't expecting it to be so small and dusty. He swore up and down it was exactly what I wanted. "I'm having a hard time with that trust thing right now. Erin, he's wearing an acid washed jean blazer. At no point in time were those ever in fashion."

"Yeah, what's that about?"

"You don't know? He said it was his lucky jacket on the phone yesterday. He was going to wear it because he knew he had found the new place for Bryant Decor."

"I'm still not sold on the new name. Why couldn't you keep the one you used in New York?"

"New and fresh, remember? I don't want to be attached to New York."

Shifting the large leather bag hanging off her shoulder, Erin raised her hand like the smartass she is. "I have a question."

"We're not in school, put your damn arm down. Why are you so weird?"

"I'm ignoring that. As your employee, don't I get a say in the name, or at least where I'll be working?"

"You're not an employee yet. I have to actually have a business for you to work for me, and location is top priority. Don't you think?"

Stan stopped right in front of a large window, clapping his arms together, which caused me to wonder how secure the stitching was on the arms of his jacket. He's a shorter man with a small, rotund belly, but the jacket was ridiculously small. If he was taller with blonde hair he would resemble the late Chris Farley doing an imitation of a fat man in a little coat.

"Out of pure curiosity, Stan, do you by chance live in a van down by the river?" A sharp pain suddenly registered in my shin as Erin kicked me. Stan seemed confused by my question, but Erin knew exactly what I was implying.

"That's an odd question, Ms. Bryant. No, I live with my wife on a lovely little ranch not too far from here. What gave you the impression I might live in a van?"

Clearing my throat, I bit the inside of my cheek to keep myself from laughing. "Nothing really. My last realtor lived in one. He said it gave him freedom." Erin suddenly excused herself to go outside. Holding her hand over her mouth, she pointed to her phone and I let out a couple of coughs. *I'm being horribly mean to this man who is desperately trying to help me.* Taking a deep breath, I pulled myself together. "Anyway, so this seems a lot smaller of a space than what I was originally looking for.

"To be honest with you, it is. But you see, it's really two spaces. The door on the back wall leads into another space. It's just a bit bigger than this one. The only problem is that you can only get to it through that door. For insurance purposes, you would need to install an additional exit for the backroom."

"Interesting. May I see it, please?"

"Of course. If you'll just follow me." Stan waved his hand toward the door as I followed behind him. The current space we were standing in was way too small to house any inventory. When I was in New York, I could have furniture brought in upon request from major designers at will. Being so far away from any major metropolitan area, I'm not going to have as much luck, so I will need to be able to store pieces as I collect them.

Stan pushed open the steel gray door. Walking in, I allowed my eyes to adjust to the bright light and dust particles floating through the air. Huge narrow windows lined the outside walls, and each window must have been at least eight feet high. Running my hands along one of the window frames I realized they didn't open. *They must've been installed for lighting purposes.* This room was at least double the size of the first one. Old, steel shelves were piled in one corner, surrounded by a few empty buckets and a broom.

"This was previously a janitorial facility. All the supplies were kept back here. A few years ago, a young man bought this place to use as a workshop, but he never moved anything in. The windows in this room were installed and he had orders for a large bay door to be put in, but he never finished it."

Using my hands, I held them in front of my face, blocking out the view of Stan, as I tried to picture exactly how I could use this space. It was an odd shaped building, but I could make it work. "Who owns it now?"

"The young man still owns it. So, what do you think?"

"It's not what I had in mind, but it has potential. It's one of the better choices, that's for sure." Slowly spinning around, I took in one last view of the two-room warehouse in desperate need of some dusting. *It's different, but maybe that's what I need,* I thought to myself. "You know what Stan? I think that jacket of yours really is lucky. I'd like to put an offer down on this place."

His face lit up as he clapped his hands together a few more times. *I think I heard the sound of stitching ripping, but I could be wrong.* "This is great. We can go over the details back at the office, or you could email me once you've thought everything through. Whichever option works best for you." Stan cleared his throat a couple of times, trying to hide the excitement in his voice, while still remaining professional.

"Email is fine. I'll make an offer and you can set it all up."

"Sounds good," Stan replied, leading me out of the backroom toward the front door, where Erin was standing outside, leaning against the large glass entrance. Tapping on the window I gave her a thumbs up, as Stan opened the door, waving me in front of him.

Erin jumped to her feet as I stepped outside. "So? Is this going to be the new place of Bryant Décor?"

"Yeah, I think so. I'm going to think it over some more, but I'm leaning toward putting in an offer. What do you think?"

"I'm not sure what you are looking for, but I like it. I saw you guys go through the other door. What were you looking at?"

"There's another room with a lot of natural lighting. It's odd for a warehouse, but it could work as a display floor," I said shrugging my shoulders. Shaking hands with Stan, I thanked him before he gave us both a friendly wave, as we walked back to my new truck. I needed something permanent after I moved out of Erin's. I borrowed her car a few times, but it was a big hassle. Not so much for me, but more for her.

Sliding onto the dark gray leather seat, I slowly turned the key in the ignition as Erin hopped in the passenger side. "I still don't understand why you let Derek talk you into a truck."

"I keep telling you, he didn't. Besides, I love this truck."

"It's not very high off the ground."

"Not every truck needs a lift kit, Erin. I wanted to be able to get in without the help of a ladder. Besides, it's fully loaded with a seat for you and a seat for me, what more could we need?"

"A ladder would be stretching it a bit. Don't you think?"

Scrunching my nose, I thought back to when Lex would lift me by my waist to help me into his truck. I could have easily gotten in on my own, I just liked when he touched me. As I backed out of the parking spot, I hesitated momentarily before turning onto the street. For a split second, I thought I saw Lex's truck pull around the back of the building. Taking a deep breath, I shook away my nerves. *I really need something else to focus on.*

"You okay? You went into DEF CON silence on me just now."

"You exaggerate way too much. I did no such thing. I'm simply being a careful driver."

Popping a piece of gum into her mouth, Erin looked over her shoulder at the warehouse as we drove past. "Careful driver? See, I thought maybe it had to do with that incredibly hot guy driving that black truck, but I must be mistaken."

"What black truck? I didn't even notice," I said, playing innocent.

"Right. Well, I'm not going to pretend like I didn't see him. You can't avoid Lex forever, sweetie. You're bound to run into one another."

Turning up the radio, I ignored Erin as I flipped through the radio stations, trying to find a song to distract me. I gave up when *Make You Miss Me* by Sam Hunt started to play. *The universe is against me,* I thought to myself. "What the hell was he doing there anyway?" Gasping, an idea suddenly occurred to me, "Do you think he's there to look at that place too? I'll tell you something, he's not getting it. I saw it first."

Erin arched her brow while inspecting her fingernails as though she could care less. "And here I thought we weren't discussing him. What are you going to do if he is looking at the warehouse? They could easily be expanding their business. You could call him and find out. Hell, give me your phone—I'll call him for you."

"Don't touch my phone. That wasn't him, and it wouldn't matter if he were. I'm putting an offer down on it as soon as I get home, so there's nothing to worry about."

"Fine, I won't say anything else. I do have one question though."

Of course she does. She wouldn't be Erin if she weren't meddling in my love life. "What's your question?"

"What bothers you more about the situation—is it that he could possibly be looking to expand, which would make him competition? Or is it because there would be a chance you would have to see him, possibly even talk to him?"

Sighing, I turned the radio down as I pulled into my driveway. "Maybe both? Does it matter? I'm still pissed."

Stepping out of the truck, Erin shut her door and leaned through the window. "Babes, it's been three months. If you're still angry, I don't think it's at him. You ended it, not him. I think he's your 'what if.'"

"My what?"

"Your 'what if.' You know, what if we would have stayed together? What if I wouldn't have walked away? What if he loved me? You're never going to get over him until you get answers."

"Thank you so much, Doctor Erin, for all of your amazing advice. Can you tell me when you got a degree in psychology? I never got an invitation to the ceremony. I would have brought you a gift."

"Fuck off, Indie. You know I'm right."

Closing my eyes, I made a mental wish. *Just ignore her and she will go away.* To my dismay, she was still standing there when I opened my eyes, giving me a knowing look. Jumping out of my truck, I closed my door and walked into my house as though she had already left. The front door closed and I could hear Erin shout from outside. "I'm right, Indie. I'm always right and you know it."

I know she's right. I'm just not willing to accept it. Tossing my keys onto the counter, I walked down the hall into my bedroom.

Boxes were still stacked in the corner. Erin kept insisting that if I finished unpacking, this place would feel like a home to me, but every time I unpacked a box I felt more disconnected from myself. *I miss New York. The control, my assistant, and the life I had was routine. Right now everything feels messy and chaotic. Maybe if I can get my new business off the ground, my routine will come back and everything will be right again. Then maybe this place will feel like home.*

Turning away from the boxes lurking in the corner, my eyes fell on the Jacuzzi tub in my master bath. *A long, hot bath with the jets on will be a great way to wash away the stress from today,* I thought to myself.

Chapter

Fourteen

LEX

Tomorrow morning I have to take Logan to physical therapy. He says it's not helping anymore, but I won't give up on him. I have sought out religions, different Gods, and tried a hundred different prayers, but not one gets answered. I guess you've got to believe in something for it to work, and I'm a little late in the game on that. *If I close my eyes right now, maybe I will get an hours worth of sleep before my dreams come for me.*

I've had the same dream for over nine years now. Nothing I do changes the outcome. I wake up knowing I will have to face my choices once again, night after night. Helping Logan is the only way I manage. Sadly, I've been using my brother, who's paralyzed from the waist down and in a wheelchair, to help myself cope. The shitty part is...I put him there.

My eyes are getting heavy. There's no use fighting this anymore. I thought to myself, before the nightmares swept in.

It always starts the same way. I'm standing by my car, thinking I own the world. I don't own shit, and I know it, but my dream doesn't care. It will still end with my parents dying in a warped steel cage, while my brother lies helpless, pulled off to the side. The only difference is that now, I'm being haunted by a beautiful girl. She holds Logan's head in her lap while she calls to me. I can't get to her in time and she fades, taking him with her while I'm left all alone.

How is it possible for someone I barely know to do this much damage? I know when I wake up in the morning, I'll reach out for her, but she won't be here. She's in New York and I doubt she even thinks of me.

There was an intense buzzing sound in my ears. Blindly reaching my hand out, I tried to find my phone. My eyes refused to open and I ended up knocking it off the nightstand. Finally managing to get my eyes to cooperate, I searched out the location of my now missing phone. Thankfully, it was hanging off the side of the stand, still connected to the charging cord. Grabbing my phone, I pulled the cord out and silenced the alarm. *Fuck. I can't believe it's already seven.* My first alarm goes off at six, which means I slept through four different alarms.

Taking a quick shower, I threw on whatever clothes I could find lying on my floor. *If I don't get downstairs to help Logan soon, we will be late.* Rushing down the steps two at a time, I stepped into the kitchen, finding my brother already dressed and sipping a cup of coffee.

"Morning, I made coffee."

"At least you're useful for something," I said sarcastically.

"That hurts, Lex. You cut me deep that time. I'm not sure how I will survive."

Tossing a muffin over to him I scoffed at his remark. "Looks like you're doing just fine to me."

"I need you to finish up that piece for the Carlson's. Pete is coming by to give me a ride to therapy today. Just so you know, I plan on making this my last visit. Nancy has been showing me exercises for me to do at home now."

"Whoa, what the hell are you talking about? Why is Pete taking you? That's my job." Logan spun his chair in a circle, completely ignoring me. *Fuck him if he thinks he can dictate orders to me outside of the shop.* "Logan, I'm your brother. I'm supposed to take care of you."

"That's it, isn't it? You're my brother—you're not my caretaker. I'm not a job."

"Where is this coming from? I take care of you because I want to."

"Coming with me you are."

"Listen, Yoda, now's not the time. It's raining. We can talk right here." He didn't listen. Instead, he headed out the side door of the kitchen, completely disregarding me. Grabbing my coffee, I followed Logan out of the house and into his office. I watched with curiosity as he sat himself behind his desk. He waved to the chair across from him.

"Logan, we don't have time—"

"Alexander. Sit," he ordered in an authoritative voice.

Pulling out the chair, I slowly slid into it as I wiped a few drops of rain from my face. Ever since the accident I have taken on the older brother role. I often forget that he's older than me, and he knows it. The only place he has a say over me is in this workshop.

Logan folded his arms in front of him. *He's using the desk and his position to make me feel small, and it's working.*

"I love you," he started.

"Okay, I love you too. Can we stop with the feelings bullshit and go? You shouldn't be late."

"I won't be. I pushed back my appointment. Like I said, Pete is taking me. He won't be here for an hour. That means we have sixty minutes to convince you to pull your head out of your ass."

"My head isn't in my ass," I replied snidely.

"No, you're right—it's in Indie's."

Sighing, I ran my hand along the back of my neck, trying to erase the tension I had building in my muscles. *Fuck him if he thinks he can fix whatever is going on in my head.* My phone suddenly chose that opportune moment to go off in my pocket. Pulling it out, I stared at the screen before silencing it. Janet needed a ride. I've been doing my best to ignore her since Indie left, but she won't give up. Eventually my guilt will eat at me and I'll pick her up from wherever she is whoring it out at.

"God damn it, give me your phone." Logan demanded.

"No."

"You are so frustrating. Why do you answer to her? I washed my hands of her. All she did was cause me pain and yet you still jump when she calls."

"What else am I supposed to do? I did this."

Logan's eyes went wide as he stared at me. *Does he not realize all of this is my fault? I'm the reason he's in that chair. I'm the reason they divorced.* Rubbing his hands over his face, he took a couple of deep breaths. "Okay, we are going to put a pin in my current thoughts and hang them up for a later time. For now, I want you to understand something—I'm supposed to take care of you. That's *my* job. As your older brother, I am putting my foot down— you will not answer to her anymore. She made her bed and she can lie in it. Besides, you're not doing her any favors by helping her."

"And when she hurts someone—what then?"

"As horrible as this is going to sound, it's her problem. If you really want to help, when she calls you, call the police. Let them deal with it. You didn't make her drink. She chose to do that all on her own."

"No, but I put you in that chair, which is why she left you. That's why she drinks."

"She drinks because she is an addict. Fuck it, if we are doing this you are going to sit in that damn chair and listen to everything I have to say, without interruption."

Sighing, I leaned back in my chair. Logan stared at me until I waved my hand in front of myself, yielding any control I had of this conversation. "Fine, let's hear it."

"One, you may have been driving the car that day, but you didn't know what was going to happen. Lex, you saved me. You pulled me from a car and ran back to it. It's not your fault. I watched you screaming in pain, trying to get me out, trying to get dad out, and it killed me. I was lying useless in a pile of dirt and there you were, being a superhero."

"You saw me?" My eyes flashed to his. *He knows?*

"We agreed on no interruptions. Shut the fuck up and listen. Two, I should have left her way before the accident. This chair was a blessing in disguise. It gave her a reason to leave. It was her way out. The drinking, the whoring around town...that's all on her. You hold no blame for that. Which brings me to number three—Indie."

"Don't bring her into this."

"What the hell don't you understand about the no talking rule? Shut. The. Fuck. Up. You brought Indie into this, and I'm glad you did. Your attention on her equaled less attention on me. I could breathe. I love you, but you can be smothering. It took me years to get you to go out on your own, and once you got used to it, it was fine. Then one night you came home and I could tell you were different. You walked around smiling like you had won a fucking prize."

"I did." I admitted. Rocking my chair back on its back two legs, I stared up at the ceiling. "What do you want from me? What is the point of this big brother intervention?" I asked.

"The point is for you to realize that I don't need you here."

My chair slammed back onto all four legs as his words raked across my skin, leaving me feeling exposed and raw. "What are you saying?"

"I'm saying, I love you...but I got this. I can take care of myself. You need to take care of you. Why did you let her go without a fight? That's not the brother I know."

"What was I supposed to do? There wasn't an 'us,' she made that clear when she was yelling at me."

"What's your point?"

"What do you mean, what's my point? I was nothing to her."

"You are a fucking moron. You were different around her. I saw the way she looked at you. There was something between you, whether she admits it or not. Call Erin, go find her. You won't be the same until you do."

Staring at the man across the desk from me, I realized just how much I had missed over the years. I had always put my focus on fixing my mistakes and making him better. What I didn't realize is that he already was. "That's your advice—call Erin? Then what? I fly to New York?"

"Yep. Now get the hell out of my office."

"What the hell?"

"I can't give you some long ass speech on how to be a man and then have you hanging around in here. I've inspired you. Now get the hell out. That's my final word."

"There's something wrong with you," I said shaking my head.

"Final word." Grinning, Logan held his palm up waving to the door. *He's really kicking me out of his office. None of this is making any sense.* Standing, I looked over my shoulder to say goodbye to him, but Logan held up a finger to his lips, shushing me. *I feel like I'm five years old and my parents have just put me in time-out.*

Stepping outside, I grabbed my phone. My finger hovered over Indie's number. *If I can make her laugh, maybe she'll give me another chance.* Instead of calling her, I sent her a text.

> **Do you play the drums?**

I waited for a reply. *Hell, she may have deleted my number by now. Is nine in the morning too early to drink? Probably. Do I care? Not really.* Heading in the house, I grabbed a beer from the fridge and started flipping through the notebook we kept in the kitchen. The phone in the barn doesn't always work right so we keep an extra copy of customer numbers in the house. It's also handy when I'm being lazy and I don't want to walk back to the barn. This was one of those times. I also wanted to avoid my brother after his 'I'm the older brother and I know better than you' speech.

Flipping through the pages, I found Derek's number. There were two numbers listed under his name. Tossing a mental coin in my head, I chose the second number, hoping it was Erin's. It rang twice before someone picked up.

"Hi, Logan." Erin's chipper voice rang in my ear.

"Um—hi. This isn't Logan, it's Lex."

"Oh! What do you want?" Her voice instantly became cold and rigid.

"I'm hoping you can help me."

"With what?"

"Indie." A high-pitched scream came across the phone, piercing my ear. "I'll take that as a yes, you can help me."

"Oh, this is great! I knew it. I told her and she was, like, 'no there's no chance.' I was, like, 'oh yeah there is.' But she didn't listen. She never does, but I was right. Ha! Take that Indigo Bryant. I knew it. I just knew it. The way she drooled over you and then the way you would look at her, like, *that*, you know?"

I have no fucking clue what she just said. "Sure. Um—so you can help me?"

"Have you called her?" she asked excitedly.

"I sent her a text."

"A text? You want me to help you and all you've done is send her a text. Lex, that's not how hearts are won."

"That's why I called you."

"You have to go to her."

"Erin, have you lost your fucking mind? I can't go to New York."

"New York? What the fuck are you talking about? She moved into a house across town. Are you drunk?"

Pinching the bridge of my nose, I let out a deep, aggravated sigh. *Why does everything have to be so fucking hard?* "She told me she was going back to New York."

"She lied to you, Lex. She's still fucking here. I can't believe her lying ass. What the fuck was she thinking—"

The line suddenly went dead. *Did she hang up on me? What the hell?* Almost immediately my phone began to ring. I answered it, confused on what had just happened.

"Hello?" I asked hesitantly.

"I'll text you her address." *Click.*

That's twice in less than a minute that I have been hung up on. Grabbing a cup of coffee, I toss my beer in the sink. *I'm not one to waste alcohol, but I need to wake up. My world is spinning out of control, and alcohol isn't going to help.* Just as I was about to set my phone down, it buzzed again.

Indie's name quickly flashed across my screen. Opening her text, I laughed.

> I'm sitting here waiting for the punch line, but you just left me hanging. Is this a serious question?

My stomach did a little flip as my fingers quickly tapped against the screen.

> Let's try this again. Do you play the drums. Cause your ass is banging.

> And there it is! I knew it was going to be awful.

> It was a good one.

> Try again.

I nervously wracked my brain trying to find another one, but I couldn't come up with anything better, so I decided to go with something worse.

I'm Mr. Right. Someone said you were looking for me?

OMG. Always so cocky.

Just with you.

Lies.

Never when it comes to you. I miss this. Do you miss me yet?

Am I supposed to?

A knife flew into my heart, twisting just a little as I read her response.

Ouch. That stings. Can I start over?

You do that a lot.

I know. Starting over.

If you were words on a page, you'd be what they call fine print.

That was so bad. It was awful. I loved it.

So back to my question...do you miss me yet?

Got to go. xx

Fuck that. I can't let her go that easily. The palpitations in my chest could probably be read on the Richter scale right now. My hand shook as I swiped my finger across the screen. It rang three times before it went straight to voicemail. *Why can't she answer her phone just once? Trying to reach her is like sending a letter to Santa...filled with lots of hope, but you never hear anything back. Maybe this wasn't my best idea.*

Fucking Logan put ideas in my head and I ran with them. What the hell am I doing? Irritation flashed through my body as I sent Logan a message letting him know that this was all his fault. *Jesus Christ.* I didn't wait for a reply. *It's not like the smug bastard has anything helpful to say anyway. Why is this so hard?* There had to be a better word than frustrated, and whatever it was, that was what I was feeling right then.

My phone buzzed across the counter in front of me, almost landing on the floor, but I was quick enough to catch it. It was a message from Erin. Peering down at the address lit up on the screen, I grabbed my keys. Catching my reflection in the mirror, I couldn't help but notice that I looked pissed. *There's no way I can show up at her front door pissed off, looking like shit.* Needing to calm myself down, I took another gulp of my coffee and headed upstairs. A quick shower and a shave were most definitely needed. *I was ready to take Logan, but I'm not ready to see her just yet. If I'm going to go over there unannounced, pouring my heart out like the dumbass that I am, I will need to have my shit together.*

Hot water cascaded over my shoulders, while I practiced what I was going to say. *I talk a big talk, but I am so full of shit. Once I see her I have no idea what's going to happen, but I guess there's only one way to find out.* Stepping out of the shower, I grabbed a towel and headed into my room

I have to see her and I'm not waiting any longer.

Chapter

Fifteen

If Erin calls me one more time to see what I'm 'up to' for the day, I'm going to stab her through my phone. It's not even nine o'clock yet. Why does she even need to know? The buzzing sound from under my pillow was an unwelcome accostment on my nerves. Grabbing my phone, I answered, "Erin, it's Friday. I have no plans and I don't intend on having any. The cloudy skies and the pitter-patter of rain on the steel roof is the anchor to my decision. There's no way I'm leaving my house. Eventually, I'll have to get out of bed, but only to use the bathroom or relocate to my couch. If you call me again I will have to start researching witches to curse you."

"It's not my fault you sleep all day. Get up and get dressed," she replied.

"I don't sleep all day. My schedule is empty because I need a day of Zen, which also includes no annoying friends disrupting my sleep."

"Fine—don't get dressed. At least I tried."

"Whatever. I'm going back to bed," I replied as my finger tapped the red button on my screen to end the call. Sometimes I really miss the satisfaction I got from slamming a phone down when I hung up on someone. Suddenly, my phone went off again while I was muttering about ways to kill her for bothering me. When I glanced down at the screen, I noticed a message from a number I thought I had deleted.

Do you play the drums?

Lex. The thought of his name alone made my stomach feel queasy. Nervous butterflies flittered around under my skin. Was this text meant for me? Maybe he had the wrong number. Maybe he's instantly regretting it. I waited for the punch line of the joke, but nothing came. Before I realized what I was doing, my fingers had already sent a response. Rolling my eyes, I read his reply. He's always so cocky and sure of himself.

When I called him out on it he responded with, "Just with you." *He's such a liar. There's no way I'm the only person to catch his attention. Even if I am, I wasn't good enough to keep it.* Letting out a snort of disgust when he asked me if I missed him, I sent a reply asking if I was supposed to. Of course I miss him, but it doesn't matter. He will always run to save her. I can't stand back and watch someone destroy themselves repeatedly. This has to end. As I was about to tell him I had to go he sent me another pick up line. This time I laughed. It was awful. Not because it made me laugh, but because it reminded me of how easily I could fall in step with him. One text and my heart was already picturing us together. Needing to distance myself from him, I decided to end our banter with a quick reply.

Got to go. xx

Lex's number lit up again on my phone, but this time he was calling me. There's no way I'm answering. I need to put some serious space between us. Between the phone calls from Erin, and the texts from Lex my brain felt fried. I hadn't even had coffee yet. *So much for my Friday in bed, but I refuse to completely give up on my day of Zen.*

While running myself a quick, hot bath, I stepped into my kitchen to make a cup of coffee. It only took a couple of seconds. I will never be able to survive if at any point I time traveled into the past. We've come too far with technology, as a society, for me to go backwards. Instant gratification is pure genius, especially when it comes to coffee.

Setting my mug down on the edge of the tub, I gently sank into the hot water after knotting my hair into a messy bun. After taking a few sips of my coffee, I closed my eyes. Concentrating on the sounds of the jets, I found myself forgetting about Lex. *My level of full Zen has now been reached.* I was half asleep when I heard someone knocking on my front door.

Fucking Erin. Stepping out of the tub, I dried myself off and pulled on a pair of black yoga pants. There was another knock as I pulled an old gray t-shirt over my head. *Why is she so impatient?* My fingers flipped the locks on my front door and I turned the handle, swinging the door open, ready to yell at her for interrupting my bath. *Holy shit.*

"You're not Erin," I said matter of fact.

"No, I'm not." Lex stood before me in a pair of dark blue wranglers hugging every inch of him just like I remembered. His tan boots were scuffed and covered with mud. Raindrops fell around him, leaving marks on my front porch steps, but my eyes refused to look up. *I know if I look at him, I'll lose my resolve.*

"What are you doing here?" I asked.

"You know why I'm here." Motioning between us with his fingers he said, "Tell me how to fix this." Stepping toward me, I instinctively stepped back, farther into my house. He was the predator and I was the prey. *I can't let him catch me.*

Looking out the door over his shoulder I could see his black truck parked in my driveway. "You shouldn't be here."

"Why? Give me one good reason and I'll go." Stepping toward me, he reached for my hand, but I pulled away. We were now both standing inside my living room. *Lex is in my house within my reach.* The sound of my heartbeat was drowning everything else around me out. Slowly turning around, I kept my eyes locked on the floor in front of me. *If he touches me, I'll break.* "Not all girls want to be saved. I don't need someone trying to rescue me or sweep me off my feet, Lex."

"Turn around. Please? I came here to see you...I need to see you."

He needs me? I broke. Turning around I looked up. His dark gray shirt was damp along his shoulders from standing in the rain. *How long was he out there?* My eyes found his, and for a split-second I let myself get lost in them. "I don't want to be saved. I don't want to get hurt either. Love is cruel, Lex. I can't do this," I tell him honestly.

"Stop." Stepping toward me, Lex wrapped his hands around my hips, pulling me closer to him. His familiar touch and scent swarm my senses, breaking down the last of the brick walls I had built around myself. "I'm not here to save you. There's no horse waiting outside for us so we can ride off into the sunset. My reasons are selfish. I came here to save myself," he admitted.

The soft cotton of his t-shirt pressed against his firm chest was distracting me from the words that were falling from his lips. My heart sped up as I felt his breath against my cheek. *This man is my weak link. No matter how many doors I try to shut, closing myself off, I'm always going to let him in.*

"I missed you," he admitted. Gently lifting my chin with his fingers his lips found mine. My fingers instinctively twisted in his hair as his body claimed mine. "No more lies. No more hiding."

Nodding my head with his lips pressed against mine, I pulled him closer to me. Nothing could be between us. Not space, not air, not even clothes. My hands started pulling at his shirt, while his lips found the spot just beneath my ear, making my knees go weak. Sliding his arms under my thighs he lifted me into the air as I wrapped my legs around him. He stumbled backwards, as his hand blindly reached out for the door. Finding it with his foot, he kicked it shut as we slammed against it. *This isn't us working anything out. No, this is us giving into whatever the fuck we are. This is animalistic. It's raw and it's fucking hot*, I thought to myself.

"Fuck." Lex moaned as he paused our movements. My back was pressed up against the door as he ran his fingers along my collarbone, making my heart skitter inside my chest.

"Don't stop. Please," I begged.

"I have to. We have got to figure this out. This thing between you and me—you can't tell me you don't feel it."

"Lex—"

"The last time you and I talked, you didn't listen. You're going to listen this time. Give me your hand."

Letting out a sigh of frustration, I slowly gave him my right hand while keeping my other hand wrapped tightly around his neck. Lex laced his fingers through mine and placed my hand over my heart. Shallow breaths fell from my lips as he pressed his forehead against mine. My heart quickened at his touch. *What is he doing?*

"You feel that?" he asked. "The instant we touch, your heart speeds up. Now feel this," he said, moving our hands, fingers still laced to press against his chest. I could feel his heart pounding against the palm of my hand, as I got lost in his eyes. "Mine does the same thing, and it's not because of how bad I want to be inside you. I mean, don't get me wrong, I fucking need to be inside of you. No—this feeling right here is because you make me feel alive."

"Lex—"

"No. You don't get a say in this. I was a mess until I met you. You invaded my dreams at night. You captured my thoughts during the day. Hell, even Logan noticed the difference in me. I'm better…because of you. You saved me. Now let me love you."

Tears brimmed my bottom lashes, but they didn't fall. Instead, I crashed my lips into his. His touch, his breath, his taste—it's everything I wanted to avoid, and everything I needed. Lex slowly lowered my legs to the floor as his fingers softly grazed my thighs. Kneeling in front of me, his fingers rolled down the waistband of my pants, while gently helping me step out of them, one foot at a time.

Our speed changed. We went from frantic and chaotic, to slow and steady. His lips pressed against the inside of my knee, slowly moving up to the crease of my thigh. Just as I was preparing myself for the onslaught of his lips against me, his lips left my skin, jumping across to my other thigh. Clenching my inner walls, I groaned in frustration. His hands slid up my waist, touching me everywhere except where I needed him most.

"You're cruel." I moaned.

"I'm finding this quite enjoyable," he admitted.

A hiss escaped my lips as he nipped at the inside of my knee. "I bet you are. I need you farther North." Slightly bending my legs, I tried to lower myself to him, hinting at where I wanted him to go. His lips traveled back up my thighs to the crease by my pelvic bone. His hot breath flashed against my skin before trailing kisses up my stomach as his hands began to cup my breasts. The ache between my thighs was deafening. I refused to wait for him.

My fingers slowly worked down my stomach, sliding between the lips of my wet pussy. A moan escaped my lips as I circled my clit, pressing against it just enough to make me want more. Lex's lips were still against my skin as he sat back on his legs, watching me. My back arched while my shoulders pressed against the door as I slid two fingers deep inside of myself, hooking them to hit the point of no return.

"Don't stop, Indie. I'm watching this and I'm taking notes. I want to see you come."

The deep sound of his voice sent chills across my skin. My breaths began to come quicker as the familiar feeling began to tingle up my spine, sending me into waves of bliss. It was the release I didn't realize I needed. It shocked me to my core, leaving me feeling spent in front of a man whose eyes were clearly telling me that he needed more.

My eyes met his gaze, as he pulled my fingers into his mouth, sucking and licking at every last drop of my orgasm. His hands pushed against my stomach, pressing my body flat against the wall. Lifting my right leg, he placed it over his shoulder as he knelt in front of me. His tongue ran up my slit as my fingers gripped his hair. Lifting my other leg, he placed it over his other shoulder. I had nowhere to go. My body was pressed up against the door, with my legs wrapped around him, as his head buried between them. All my weight was on his shoulders as he licked and nipped at my clit, sucking it into his mouth before swirling his tongue around it. *Fuck me!*

I once saw something like this in a porn. Both people looked uncomfortable as fuck, and everything looked so forced and unnatural. However, nothing about this was awkward or unnatural. I was enjoying every bit of it, and his fingers twisting and pulling at my nipples let me know he was too. Suddenly, I was lifted into the air and the front of my body fell over his shoulders.

"Couch or bed? Tell me where to go."

"Bed—down the hall."

"Good choice." The sting of his hand across my ass caused me to yelp as he carried me down the hall, kicking open doors until he found my bedroom. Slowly lowering me to the floor, he turned me to face the bed. His hands gently lifted my shirt from my body, leaving me to stand completely nude in front of him.

"I need you," I begged.

"Hush—don't move." All I could hear was the unsnapping of the buttons on his jeans. A loud thump followed a swift movement of air behind me, causing goosebumps to ripple across my skin. His lips found my neck as he nipped at the spot just below my ear. A shiver rolled down my spine in response to his hot touch.

"I want you to walk to the end of the bed and bend over, while spreading your legs apart for me. Don't bend your knees, keep them straight," he ordered.

Following his directions, I turned my head to the side with my cheek resting on my mattress. His hands gripped my hips, pulling me against him. "I love you, Indie," he whispered. Closing my eyes, I reveled in the meaning of his words. Slowly, the hard length of his cock pressed against my slit, spreading me open to him. He moaned as he slid into me.

Begging for more, I whispered, "Again."

His fingers tightened their hold on my body, gripping me and pulling me harder against him as he thrust into me again. Pressing my chest farther into the mattress, I arched my back as he slammed into me. Moans and the sound of skin on skin filled the room around us. A feeling of bliss overcame me as he collapsed on top of me.

I was vaguely aware of my body being moved, and the sound of his short breaths against my ear as he wrapped his body around me while I drifted off to sleep. The soft caress of his fingers gently stroking my arm slightly stirred my dream-like state.

"Indie," he whispered.

"Hmm?"

"I need you to know this wasn't what I came over here for." Lex's fingers stilled as he rolled me onto my back. Brushing the loose strands of hair from my face, he kissed my forehead. "That sounded all wrong—I came here because there was no chance I was letting you go. You make everything better—more better."

Snickering, I questioned his lack of grammar. "More better? That's a horrible use of English."

"It's not my fault. You've exhausted me and I can't think of the word I need. You make me more than just better. It's more better. You know like—better, but it's so much more—more better."

Shaking my head, I let out another laugh. "More better? We need to get you a thesaurus."

"Listen, city girl, I'm trying to pour my heart out over here and confess my love for you and you're correcting my grammar. You're ruining the moment."

"My apologies. Please continue. I believe you were saying I was *more better*, or was it that I made you more better?" Giggles erupted from my chest as he straddled me, pinning my wrists above my head. "What are you doing?" I asked between my soft laughter.

"Are you going to let me finish now?"

"I thought you just did. Are we going for round two?"

"You are something else." Leaning down, Lex placed a soft kiss on my lips before pushing himself off the bed. "You and I still have things to talk about. As long as you're naked I'm going to be distracted. Get dressed."

Lex was standing in the kitchen, attempting to make coffee, when I walked in behind him wearing my favorite sweats. His hand smacked the top of my coffeemaker while muttering under his breath. Pushing him away with a bump of my hip, I opened it and popped in a coffee pod. His brow furrowed as he watched me reach for a coffee mug and place it underneath the dispenser. "You're making this harder than it is. When the lights turn blue, press the button for whatever size cup of coffee you want."

"This is not coffee. This is some kind of voodoo latte maker."

"I suggest you get used to it. Me and the voodoo latte maker have a serious relationship. No one gets between us. We made a vow."

"Indie, you're trying to be funny and cute right now, but it's not working. The vow you need to be worried about is the one you are going to be making to me."

Shit. Is he talking about marriage? Is there another kind of vow? The palpitations in my chest increased ten-fold as I tried to figure out what he meant. Sweat trickled down my neck and my skin began to itch. *Am I having an allergic reaction?* I wondered.

Reaching for the wall with my hand, I steadied myself as I slowly walked over to the tall, French style windows, looking out into the backyard. My breathing eased as the cool glass pressed against my skin. Sinking to the floor, I tried to make sense of what he was telling me.

"Hey, what's going on? Indie, you're white as a ghost."

"I need a minute." I mumbled, trying desperately to regulate my breathing.

Leaning down next to me, Lex handed me a fresh cup of coffee. Taking a few sips, I kept my head pressed against the cool glass. My eyes closed as his fingers gently stroked my back. I didn't want to find his touch calming, but I couldn't help it. "I'm sorry, I don't do any of this very well," I admitted.

"You and I need to talk. I scared you a bit I think. Come on." Holding out his hand he took my coffee and helped me up from the floor. Linking my fingers with his, I led him to my oversized, dark gray couch. Lex sat down as I grabbed a pillow, tucking it in my lap as I sat next to him. Tracing the light blue pattern with my fingers, I tried desperately to organize my thoughts.

"What is this? What are we?" I asked, desperately searching for answers.

"I was hoping you'd tell me. It took me longer than it should have to realize how much I hurt you when I left that night."

"It wasn't just because you left. I wanted you to see what I saw—and you couldn't. When I told you I loved you and you threw it back at me, that was my breaking point."

"I'm sorry. I thought I was doing the right thing."

"And now?" I asked.

"Now I'm sitting on what I hope is my girlfriend's couch, asking her to take me back. I'm not perfect. Self-created damage surrounds me everywhere I go. You saw Logan, you know what I did. I couldn't handle you loving me. You didn't need me."

"I've never needed anyone but myself. It's been years since I was dependent on anyone and even then, I didn't like it."

"I don't know what to say to that." Not knowing how to reply, I stared blankly at the man in front of me.

Sighing, Lex raked his hands over his face. "Logan needs me. I thought Janet needed me. When I help them, when I do right by them, I feel like I'm needed. It's my fault that things ended up the way they did—it was only right that I fix them. At least that's what I thought. However, it seems you and Logan feel differently."

"When you help Logan, you do it out of love. That's different. You're helping Janet out of guilt and it's not helping anyone. Neither of you are facing your problems. She's not going to forgive you, and what happened to her is not your fault. You can't get forgiveness when you've done nothing wrong. You and I can't happen if she's in the picture. I won't sit by and watch you hurt yourself over and over again." The hurt that registered in his eyes sank my stomach.

"I haven't driven her home since that night," he admitted. "She's called me and I gave her lame excuses, but I didn't go to her."

Nodding my head, I said, "I have some requests if we are going to make this work. The first one is that you have to delete her number and stop going to her rescue. She's a plague and she's going to consume anything and everything good about you. Let her go."

"Done."

"The second...I want you to go to therapy. You need someone to talk to instead of keeping all of this inside, it's not healthy."

"No. I can remove her from my life, but I don't need therapy—I need you. You can be my therapy."

I can be his therapy? He wants me to save him, I thought in realization. "I can't save you from yourself or your past, Lex."

"No, but you can make my future so much better. More better," he said with a grin.

Rolling my eyes, I shake my head at his horrible use of grammar. *Apparently not only does he need a therapist, but some grammar courses as well.* "More better isn't a thing."

"It is with you. What's your issue with Cupid?"

"He's a drunk, miniature deity that flies around armed with arrows. He has no clue what he is doing."

"I don't know…he made me see you. I wasn't looking to meet anyone, and yet there you were, degrading people on their choice of clothing attire in bar."

Tossing the pillow in my lap to the floor, I found myself yelling at him. "Really? So, explain my family. Go on—explain how the fuck they happened. Using people as pawns and taking advantage of them is not what I was told love was, but yet it's all I ever saw."

"Whoa! Where the fuck is this coming from?"

"Cupid ruined my family!" I shouted. "My dad was a womanizer with eyes for everyone except my mom. She couldn't handle it so she became a drunk, using my younger brother and I as pawns in the 'who loves you more' game. Then they started blatantly cheating on one another just to hurt the other person. When I was younger, my mom would tell me how they met. I thought fairy tales were real, but as I grew older I realized what love meant. Love meant people hurting one another just to make the other person feel pain. Love isn't fair. It destroys entire families.

Even my brother fell for it. Now he's getting divorced after his wife caught him cheating for the second time. It's all a bunch of lies," I said breathlessly.

"You're describing hate. That's not what love is."

"And yet you hurt me." I accused.

"That's not hate…and you lied to me. You never went to New York."

"So where does that put us on the love spectrum?"

Reaching for my hand, Lex brought it to his lips. "That just means I'm crazy in love with you."

Sighing, I gave in to the man beside me as I spun my body on the couch so I could lay my head in his lap. "Should we talk about something else now?" I asked, feeling completely drained.

"Sure. You know I finally broke down and let Logan expand the company. We are doing great, but he wants to be able to display everything. He's hoping it will bring in new buyers." His voice dropped as he mentioned the possibility of expanding.

"That's good. Why do you make it sound so awful?"

"I can't find a space I like. I looked at a place last week. It would've been perfect, but when I went to make an offer, the buyer said they already had one and there was no sense in them looking at more. Who does that?"

Oh my God! That was him! I thought to myself. "Apparently a really smart seller. I mean, if the first offer was perfect, why take your chances on something else?"

"I could use you on my side for this. Get angry or at least give me a little sympathy. I finally let Logan talk me into expanding and the warehouse I wanted gets taken. I wanted to meet with the other buyer, but my realtor said that would be impossible. Besides, I found out last night that the seller accepted the other offer."

"Was it a small warehouse with a larger connected one in the back?"

"Yeah, it had these large windows. How did you know?" he asked, slightly confused.

"Lex, I love you and all, but that buyer is incredibly smart. You should just walk away from it. The warehouse isn't yours. It's time to move on." His hand stilled on my arm as his eyes narrowed their gaze on me. Rolling onto my back, I smiled sweetly up at him. "Just ask Stan and his lucky jacket."

Shaking his head back and forth, Lex gave me a grin most people would run from. "How do you know Stan? And I would choose your words carefully."

"Stan? Oh, we go way back. He's one of my closest friends. In fact, he showed me that exact same warehouse. Thanks to his lucky jacket, I put a bid on that very warehouse you are talking of so fondly. If it weren't for you, I wouldn't have known the seller had accepted. I haven't checked my email this morning because I've been otherwise occupied. So thank you for that."

"You! Don't you smile at me like that. You owe me a warehouse, city girl," he said playfully.

"I don't owe you anything."

"Indie, you owe me. Pay up." Laughter escaped me as he lifted me up, tossing me on the cushion beside him. "Pay up."

"Nope, it's mine. If you're nice, I'll share it with you, for a small fee of course."

"No fees. Give me what's mine." Crawling over me, Lex spread my legs, making room for his large frame to hover over mine.

"How about an even exchange?" I proposed. "I get the warehouse and you get me. Seems fair to me."

"No more lies or running?"

"I'll stay right here. What about Janet?"

"Fuck her—I got you." His lips softly fell to mine. Our tongues danced as our hands slowly pulled at one another. Lex took his time inspecting every inch of my body. It was slow, sweet, and left my heart bursting at the seams with love for him.

Whatever comes between us, I know we will work it out. I can help save him from himself and he can teach me to love. We're too good together to let this go.

Chapter

Sixteen

Fall had faded into winter, and Olivia was standing next to me with a blue handkerchief with a little bow at the top tied into her hair. The knees of her overalls were covered in dust from playing outside in the small patch of brown grass behind the warehouse. Her bottom lip started to stick out as she held out her hand, wanting what was in mine. Not able to tell her no, I gently hand her the broom I had been using for the past hour. "Your daughter is spoiled rotten, Erin."

"Don't you dare put that blame on me. I'm not the one who took her shopping for her birthday, buying any toy she pointed at."

"For your information, I told her no on a few things. She's very demanding. It wasn't my fault.

"She's one and a half, Indie. She can't demand anything."

"Oh yes she does. Look at how she took my broom." I said, putting a hand on my hip as I pointed to where Olivia was walking. She tripped herself with the long, red handle, but she was determined to drag it behind her.

"She pouted and you gave in." Erin said with a smirk. "You have no backbone when it comes to her. I worry for any future children you may have."

"No need, I'm not having kids."

"You say that now, but I bet if Lex asked, you wouldn't hesitate to say yes."

"I don't think so. He brought kids up the other day and we both tip-toed around the subject. It's not something either of us are ready for."

"You would make a great mom. Just think how amazing it would be."

Just as I was about to reply, the bell above the front door rang, letting me know someone had just walked in up front. Peeking at the feed from the camera I saw it was Lex. "Crap, it's him. Do not mention the baby word near him. I mean it, Erin. It's only been two months since we got back together. Please don't make him run."

Erin looked up at me as she finished stacking the papers on her desk. "Sweetie, he loves you. It's a disgusting display every time he sees you. He acts like he hasn't seen you in years, even if you've only been apart for minutes. There's absolutely nothing you can do to make him run," she said sincerely.

"My heart knows you're right, but my mind has a hard time accepting it. Please, just let it go," I begged.

Holding her hands up into the air in front of her, she made a cross over her chest. "I won't say a thing. Now go in there before he comes looking for you, and I get stuck watching you two make out."

Laughing, I pushed open the door to the main room where I kept my office and a few pieces of furniture on display. When I walked in, Lex was messing with the angle of the armoire in the corner that he had built. Every time he comes in he adjusts it to stand flat against the wall. And every time he leaves, I fix it so it stands angled in front of the corner. *He just needs to give it up. Not everything needs to fit together squarely.*

As he stepped back from the armoire, admiring the angle it was now sitting at, he caught a glimpse of me out of the corner of his eye. "Why do you keep moving this? I built it, I should know how it's supposed to be displayed."

"You built it—that doesn't give you a right to say how it looks in a room. That's why I'm the interior decorator. It's what people pay me to do."

"Have it your way. Just come over here so I can reach you."

Slowly walking toward him, I leaned up on my toes, sweetly placing a kiss on his cheek. Grabbing my waist, he spun me around as I laughed hysterically, while he placed kisses on my neck. "God, I needed you," he whispered into my ear.

"I just saw you this morning. It's only been six hours."

"That's too many. You know, if you would move in with me I could see you whenever I wanted."

"Lex, we've been over this. Whether I move in with you or not, I will still be gone during the day. We have jobs, babe, and I can't be with you all the time. Besides, what does Logan say to your idea of me moving in?"

Wrapping his arms around my waist, he pulled me closer to him. "Logan has no say in it. As of this morning he's no longer living with me. He found a house with a ramp and an accessible kitchen. As of ten o'clock this morning it was officially his."

"What? Why didn't you tell me? Why didn't either of you tell me?"

"I wanted to surprise you. I can't ask you to officially move in with me with my older brother still lurking around. Now that he's gone, the house is empty. I'm lonely, Indie. Move in with me."

"How can you possibly be lonely? You haven't even been alone for a day yet."

Giving me his best puppy dog eyes, he replied, "I know—and it scares me. I love you. Move in with me. Just say yes."

"Lex—"

"Consider it payment for stealing this place from me."

Pushing my hands against his chest, I challenged him with an arch of my brow. "I didn't steal anything. I bought this fair and square. Besides, I thought we were even."

"We were, until I decided we weren't. To be even, I would need all of you, and that's impossible with you living somewhere else. Move in with me."

"You are an awful negotiator."

"Is that a yes?" he asked with the biggest grin on his face.

"Yes. I'll move in with you…on one condition."

"What's that?"

"You leave the furniture where I put it."

"Deal." His lips found mine as he lifted me from the floor, carrying me over to the desk. My hands twisted in his hair as his fingers began to slide under my shirt.

"Seriously? You two need to get ahold of yourselves. There are young eyes here. My daughter doesn't need to learn where babies come from by accidently walking into an amateur porn demonstration. I don't want to see it either," Erin stated as she walked into the room.

Sighing, Lex pulled back down my shirt and helped me off my desk. "Why is she always here?"

"*She* is standing right here and *she* can hear you. And for your information, I'm here because this is where I work. When I took the job, I was unaware of the make-out sessions that would frequently take place. Thankfully, it's time for me to go. I'll see you two later tonight. Indie, I expect details," Erin said as she walked out the front door with Olivia on her hip.

"Details?" Lex asked in confusion.

Looking up, I stared back at the man who was now questioning my friend. "She's crazy. It's best to ignore her."

"Noted. How much longer do we have to be here? I want to go home and fuck you like crazy."

"All I have to do is shut off the lights and lock the doors. If you help me it will be quicker," I stated with a wicked smile. The words barely fell from my lips before he took off to the back room. Laughing, I grabbed my purse, shut down my laptop, and turned off the lights in the front room. As I stepped outside to wait for Lex, my eyes took in my new endeavor. Erin was right about the name. Bryant Décor wasn't working. Lex suggested maybe a nickname or something that was closer to my heart. I needed the name to grab my attention, and since Lex was currently hogging it all, it only seemed fitting to use the nickname he gave me. Just like that, City Girl Designs was born.

Spinning my keys around my finger, I watched Lex as he raced toward the front door, composing himself just before he walked through it. "Why aren't you in your truck? Why are we still standing here?"

"Calm yourself! Sweet lord, you're acting like you're dying. I have to lock the door behind you. I'll meet you at my place."

"You mean your old place? You live with me now."

Letting out a soft sigh as I locked the door, I turned around to face the anxious man in front of me. "I can't shower at your place. I need clean clothes, my makeup bag, my shoes, and basically all of my things."

"It's our place. We need to get your things over to *our place* as soon as possible, city girl."

"I'll work on it. What time are we meeting up with Derek and Erin?"

"He said after seven. That gives us plenty of time."

Rolling my eyes, I gave him a quick kiss on the cheek before hopping in my truck.

Two pairs of flats, three pairs of heels, two pairs of knee high boots, including one that laced up my thighs, one pair of ankle boots with a split that folded along the top of the zipper, three pairs of sandals, and two black clutches were lying, spread out at the end of my bed. *There's no way I can fit them all in my small luggage bag without bending or creasing them. It's not going to happen.* Deciding to switch out my suitcases, I grabbed the larger one for my shoes and started packing them, making sure to leave out a pair of boots for tonight.

Lex walked in as I was packing the smaller suitcase with a few of my t-shirts, two pairs of black yoga pants, a couple pairs of jeans, and a sweater, just in case it got cold enough to wear it. My fingers slid along the top of my dresser as I started sorting through the pile of mismatched panties and bras I had laid out earlier.

"The big bag is for your shoes?" Lex questioned.

"Yep."

"And you're going to use this tiny one for your clothes?" he asked, even more puzzled.

"Yeah. My clothes I can iron and sort out later. I can't do that with my shoes. That's not even all of them, those are just my favorites."

"You have a problem."

"No, I don't. I worked hard for my money and I will spend it any way I like. If shoes make me happy, then I'm buying fucking shoes. You need to get over it."

Lex slid his arms around my waist, pulling me closer to him as my gaze caught his in the mirror. "If you want shoes, buy shoes. I don't care. Which ones are for tonight?"

"The black leather ones with the bows on the back."

"They look long. What else do I get to see you in?"

"That dark purple dress hanging in the corner. The back is completely open, so I'm wearing my black leather jacket with it until I get hot. Then I can just take it off."

Leaning over my shoulder, he placed a hot, searing kiss under my ear. My thighs clenched as I fought off the urge to give into him. "Indie, get dressed. We need to go."

"Fine. I'll zip these up and you can put them in the truck while I finish getting ready."

"Nope. I'm going to stay right here and watch you get dressed. Dress and boots."

Nodding my head, I walked toward the corner where my dress was, as Lex made himself comfortable at the end of my bed. "You'll have to take off those sweats you have on. Do you need help?"

"You want a show? I'll give you one, but you can't touch me. My makeup and hair are already done, and you're not going to make a mess of me before we leave." Slowly pushing at the band of my sweats, I stepped out of them, revealing the black lace panties I had underneath.

A smile spread across his face as I walked towards him. Reaching behind Lex, I grabbed the boots and slowly slid them up my legs. His eyes followed the slow movements as my fingers pulled the inside zippers up toward my thighs, stopping just a few inches above my knees. Slightly bending over, I felt for the tiny black bows at the top of my boots; one in front and one in back. *I know if I were to face him right now, he would be ready to attack every inch of me.*

Doing my best to avoid his gaze, I walked over to the corner and gently pulled the deep purple dress from its hanger. Lifting it above my head, I allowed the dress to slowly fall over my head and down my shoulders. The dress was short, but long enough to cover anything Lex would consider to be 'his'. The sound of footsteps behind me let me know how close he was to me.

"I think you forgot something?"

"No, I don't think so. Panties, boots, and the dress—what else is there?"

The soft stroke of his fingers up my spine sent shivers exploding across my body. "I think you forgot a bra."

"I can't wear one with this dress. It falls too low in the back and the halter ties around my neck. Could you tie it for me?"

Lex gently grabbed the two slim pieces of purple lace I was holding behind my neck. Tightening the strings, he tied a knot, followed by a small bow at the base of my neck. "The only way you're getting out of this dress is if I cut those strings."

"Stop it! You're not cutting anything—you can untie them later. Are you ready?"

"Yes, but I'm ready for something completely different."

"Later. Come on, Erin will be waiting on us. Drinks are on them tonight and I plan on taking full advantage of it."

"That dress is making me crazy. Put your jacket on."

A soft giggle fell from my lips as I pulled on my black leather jacket. Linking my fingers with his, I grabbed my clutch while dragging him from the room. *If I let him, he would keep me in here all night, and as fun as it would be, I really want to go dancing with Erin.*

It was supposed to be a girl's night, but the boys pouted until we gave in. *Whether they are with us or not, I'm still going to be with my best friend, drinking and dancing all night, to celebrate the opening of City Girl Designs.*

Chapter

Seventeen

Lex threw a temper tantrum most of the drive over to the bar. He couldn't get over how high my boots were and how short my dress was. It was only the two of us in his truck, yet he still insisted I covered my legs with the blanket in the back of the truck. He swore up and down people could see through the truck windows. *I have no idea what the big deal is, it's not like I can't handle myself. It's just a pair of boots and a dress.*

Erin was already sitting at the table with a drink waiting for me when we arrived. *I love the way she gets me,* I thought to myself. Plopping down on a barstool beside her, I took a gulp of the cool liquid in front of me. "I really needed this. Thank you. He's got his knickers all twisted over my outfit. I had to use a blanket in the truck because 'someone might be able to see me.' It was ridiculous."

"I can only imagine. Those are definitely some 'come fuck me' boots. I'm married and straight, but my eyes are still all over you. You look hot as hell in those. Legs for days."

"I haven't worn them in a while. They were my go-to pair when I would go to the club back in New York. I thought I'd break them in a bit, and they certainly got Lex's attention. That's for sure."

"Indie, they have everyone's attention. Every person in this bar watched you walk in and take your seat. I think the guys behind us are still watching. Lex is going to flip shit if he catches them."

Shrugging my shoulders, I took another sip of my Whiskey Sour as Lex walked over with a beer in his hand. "Those legs—you're killing me. Can you at least keep them under the table?"

"Nope, but if you're good, maybe later they will be under you." Slamming back the rest of my drink, I grabbed Erin's hand and dragged her to the hardwood floor in front of the band. I didn't know the words to the songs they were playing, but it didn't make a difference, I was going to dance to them anyway.

Erin and I were both sweating and needed a break. Grabbing my hand, she pulled me back over to the table so we could cool off with another drink. "Derek, we need more drinks. It's a lot hotter than I thought."

Derek cocked his head to the side as he processed our request. Kissing Erin on the forehead he stood, and headed to the bar, taking Lex with him. My eyes quickly scanned the room. *There's a lot less plaid than the first time I came here. Of course, it could have just seemed that way since I felt so out of place then.* Pulling at the sleeves of my jacket, I slipped it off my shoulders and laid it on the table in front of me. It was ridiculously hot.

Erin's eyes went wide as I turned to face her. "Indie—you are missing the entire backside of your dress."

"I'll have you know, *mother*, I bought it this way."

"Does Lex know you're missing half of your dress?"

"Why is everyone so concerned with what I'm wearing? I work hard to keep myself fit and toned. It's my money that purchased this dress. It's my body and I'll put whatever the hell I want on it."

"Alright. I'm sorry I said anything. Are you okay?" she asked, her voice laced with concern.

Taking a deep breath, I pulled my long hair over my shoulder, revealing more of my skin. "Yes. No—I don't know."

"What happened? You're getting defensive and that's not like you, unless you feel cornered."

"Lex asked me to move in with him and I said yes. What if it's too soon? What if he tries to change me or, God forbid, he hurts me? What do I do then? Now, all of a sudden, he's concerned with what I'm wearing. He doesn't own me."

"Sweetie, I love you, but this has nothing to do with what you are definitely *not* wearing. This is you freaking out because you've given away some of your control. You wouldn't have said yes if you weren't ready."

"I know. I just have a lot of what ifs. I don't know how to do this."

"Why don't you start with just letting go a bit. Moving in with anyone is a big change. It will take time to get used to. He doesn't want to control you, either. Have you seen yourself? You went from a t-shirt and ripped jeans, to 'come fuck me' boots with a dress that's being held together by a string around your neck. Lex loves it, even if he's worried about other people looking. Just ignore him."

Nodding my head, I smiled as Lex walked back over with my drink in his hand. He snaked one arm around my waist as he leaned over my shoulder and whispered in my ear, "You took off your jacket."

"I did. It was hot."

"What if other people try to touch you? Fuck! Now I want to touch you."

"They can't and you already are."

"Damn straight I'm touching you. You're going home with me and no one else."

"I was always going home with you. It's where I live," I replied with a smile.

Spinning me around, his lips met mine, while his hands gently cupped the sides of my face. "Fuck yeah you do. You wanna dance with me?"

"Okay."

Leading me to the dance floor, he kept one arm wrapped around my waist, making sure I was close to his side. My arms found their way around his neck as my body pressed up against him. *He's so much taller than me when we dance like this.* Looking down, I carefully placed my boots on top of his. Once I made sure we were matched up, my eyes found his, as I pulled his lips down to mine. *Whiskey, salt, and Lex are my new favorite flavor.* We danced slowly, completely off beat, with our bodies pressed tightly together. Breathing in the scent of his cologne, my fingers tightened around his neck.

"You okay?" I asked.

"Yeah, I'm kind of hoping you take me home soon, but can I get one more drink before we go?"

"Indie, you can have whatever the fuck you want. I love you." Blush crept up onto my cheeks, as he linked our fingers, leading us back to the table where Derek and Erin were sitting. "Stay with Erin, I'll be right back." Smiling, I nodded my head at him. I was staring down at my fingers when Erin bumped her shoulder into mine.

"You really love him, don't you?"

"Yeah. When I left to come here, it was to start over. I never planned on him."

"The best kinds of plans are the ones we don't know about."

"When did you get so wise?"

Laughing, Derek slapped the edge of the table. "Wise, my ass. That wise quote was from a fortune cookie she had last night at dinner. What were your lucky numbers, babe?"

"Fuck you, Derek. I don't remember what they were. Indie, ignore him. It doesn't matter where the wisdom came from. It applies to the situation, so just go with it."

My eyes were scanning the groups of people scattered throughout the bar as I ignored the two weirdos beside me who were still arguing over the meaning of fortune cookies and whether they were accurate or not. A shadow suddenly passed under the neon lights of the windows along the side of the bar, and my eyes immediately followed it to the front door. As it entered the bar, anger seared across my skin. Grabbing Erin's arm, I nodded toward the person the shadow belonged to.

"What is your problem?" Erin asked in concern.

"Erin, just shut up and look." I replied. Turning her head toward the direction I was now pointing, her mouth fell open. "Oh my God! What the fuck is she doing here?"

We both watched as Janet walked over toward a rather large, burly man sitting next to one of the pool tables. *Holy shit. This cannot be happening.* Looking up toward the bar, I searched for Lex. His back was to them as he paid for ours drinks.

"Um, Indie, maybe we should go," Erin said, looking from me to Janet and back again.

"Yeah, I'm ready. Don't say anything to Lex, he hasn't noticed them yet. I think it would be better if he didn't. Let's just finish our drinks and go."

Before Lex could make it back to our table, Janet spotted him. *Fuck.* Thankfully luck must have been on my side when I caught Lex's attention as I rushed toward him.

"Hey, what's all this? You okay?"

"I just...I have a headache. Can we go?"

"Yeah, let me set these drinks down and we'll grab your jacket. You sure it's just a headache?"

"Yep. I just want to go." Taking my drink from Lex, I followed him to our table where Erin and Derek were getting ready to go.

"You guys are leaving too, huh?"

I knew Erin was awful at keeping secrets or hiding things from people, so I instantly regretted asking her not to mention Janet. Her nervous head bounced around like the bobble headed Jesus on my ex-boyfriend's dashboard, as her eyes flew back and forth between Lex, Janet, and me. I've often wondered if you stare at someone hard enough if they can feel it. The glare I was giving Erin had no effect on her whatsoever. Lex, however, managed to sense my unease. Turning around, he found what Erin couldn't help but look at.

"A headache, huh?" he asked knowingly.

"To be honest she's more of a migraine." Lex didn't find my reply funny at all. He was staring straight at me as though I had committed a crime. "I don't want to ruin our night and that's exactly what she will do. Let's just go."

"Yeah, okay." The somber tone of his voice pulled on my heart. He didn't have to mention the guilt he carried, I could see it shackled to his back, weighing him down as we stepped away from the table. *I'm going about this all-wrong...why should we have to leave?*

"You know what, no—we're not going to leave because she walked in. If anyone should leave, it should be her. Look at what she's doing to you. This isn't fair to you or to us. She's the one with the problem. I'm going to finish my drink." Grabbing my glass from the table, I took two rather big gulps, letting the Whiskey warm its way through my body. Lex was watching me with his head tilted to the side as a lopsided smile appeared on his face.

"Indie, you make me crazy."

Shrugging my shoulders, I took another sip before reaching up on my toes to place a kiss on his chin. "That was supposed to be on your lips, but I can't reach them."

"Let me help you fix that." Leaning down, his hand gently grasped the side of my face as he brought his lips down to mine. The taste of him swirling around in my mouth, along with the Whiskey was incredible.

My arms were wrapped tightly around his waist when I heard a screech I could have gone my entire life without hearing again.

Pointing at us, Janet turned to the burly man and said, "See? I told you. Kick their asses."

Taking a deep breath, I turned to face Janet. Her fake leather skirt was so short, I was almost certain I could make out the pattern on her panties. She was wearing, what I assume was a G-string, due the strings peeking out of the top of her skirt. The netted white shirt she was wearing over her yellow tank top was the icing on the cake. If a person were to Google the word classy, Janet would be the exact opposite of whatever they found.

Not paying attention to where she was pointing, the man asked, "Who was messing with you, woman?" The burly man looked toward me as a laugh coughed from his cigarette infested lungs. "Woman, get the hell off me. No one is worth that kind of *trouble*," he replied.

Grinning, I recalled the last time we met. *He remembers me. Smart man.*

"But Ray—"

"Don't 'but Ray' me. No blowjob is worth this. I'd rather stick my dick in an electrical socket. Woman, you've lost your damn mind if you think I'm going to handle her. No fucking way in hell." Shaking his head, the man nodded toward me before walking back over toward the pool table. Janet was pulling and pawing at him the entire way. Eventually, he pushed her off of him hard enough that she fell to the floor, taking a couple of chairs with her.

"Indie, did he just imply she was going to pay him with a blowjob to kick our asses?" *Leave it to Erin to try and decipher the crazy scene that just took place.*

"I honestly have no clue. The only thing I caught was that he preferred electrical outlets to the STD's lurking in her mouth." Laughing, Erin and I both shivered from the thought. Turning around, ignoring the drunken woman crawling around on the floor, I slammed back the rest of my drink. Setting my glass down I looked up at Lex. "Finished my drink and I'm ready to go."

"Thank God." he said, linking my fingers with his as he led us toward the front door. *I hate how close together these tables are. They always leave such a narrow passageway it's hard to get through without bumping into someone or something.* I was half a step behind Lex when something pushed me forward, knocking me off balance into one of the empty tables.

"What the hell?" I shouted. Turning around, I found Janet standing in front of me. The crook in her nose matched the evil smile under her smeared lipstick.

"You dumb bitch. I figured you'd have left his ass by now. I wouldn't be caught dead with him in a car. He's dangerous, you know."

"Are you saying he's only good enough to drive people around when they're drunk? You had no problem calling him for a ride home whenever you finished whoring yourself out. I suggest you walk away. I bit my tongue the last time, but I won't do it again." Lex pulled at my arm, trying to get me to follow him, but I refused to move. *Janet needs to be put in her place, once and for all.*

"Aww, how cute. Looks like he doesn't want you talking to me. Did he tell you he loves you yet? That's a death sentence, you know." Janet swayed on her feet before steadying herself by gripping onto a chair. "He hurts the ones he loves. He'll destroy you. Just ask his mother. Oh wait, you can't, and why is that?" she asked, glancing over at Lex.

I ignored the people calling my name, as well as the pulls on my body. My focus was on the crooked, freckled nose in front of me. Everything slowly faded around me as I pulled my arm back.

CRACK! The fear in her eyes as they rolled back in her head is a moment I will always hang on to. Her body slumped to the floor as I was lifted into the air.

The bartender was yelling at Lex to get me out of the bar. People were moving tables, as others were being yelled at to move. For being just over five feet tall I packed quite the punch. Janet was out cold, sprawled across the bar floor. She got what she deserved. My only regret was not being able to do it again.

The lights in the bar faded as Lex carried me, draped over his shoulder, outside to the bed of his truck. Setting me down he grabbed my hand and looked me over. "I remember doing this before. Is this going to be a frequent occurrence with you?"

"No, but she pissed me off. She was intentionally trying to hurt you." Placing my hand in his, I looked up into his dark blue eyes. "I don't want you to hurt anymore. She only made things worse. You wanted to be saved—that's me saving you. I won't let her hurt you anymore."

"Indie, that's not what I meant when I said I wanted you to save me. You just being you, loving me the way you do, that's how you saved me."

Softly pulling at his shirt, I brought his lips down to mine. "I love you."

"I know. I love you too. What I don't love is having to carry you out of a bar because you can't control your temper."

"But—"

"I don't care what she said. She's not worth hurting yourself over. If I'm not mistaken, I believe that's what you were trying to tell me that night you referred to her as a cancer. Am I right?"

"You're right. I'm sorry."

It was at that precise moment Erin and Derek walked over. I closed my eyes, instantly regretting saying the words loud enough for her to hear. "Lex, you are going to need to save this moment. She never admits to being wrong. I've only heard her say that one other time and I have it recorded on my phone." Laughing, Erin kicked at a piece of gravel near the tire of Lex's truck. "I'm sure he's lectured you on what a horrible decision you made back there, but I want it to be known that I'm on your side. She's an awful person. I loved the way her head rolled back. I think you shocked everyone in that bar, except me. Maybe I should tell Lex about all the fights you used to start at school."

"Erin, now would be a good time for you to shut up," I stated firmly.

Chuckling to himself, Lex gently placed a soft kiss on my forehead. "You were a fighter, huh? I would be lying if I said I couldn't picture you in that way. After seeing Janet fall like that, I have no doubt in my mind that you used to kick a lot of ass."

"Not a lot. There were a few girls I got into an argument with, after I drew some penises on their friend's car. In all fairness, they were dick flowers, so if anything, it was an artistic choice."

"She's not lying. Indie was quite the badass," Erin confirmed.

Sticking my tongue out at Erin, I flipped her off. "I'll have you know, I'm still a badass. Did you not just see what happened? Case in point."

"Right. Well, you two can bicker about Indie's badass status later. Right now, I'm taking her home to ice that hand," Lex said, helping me down from the bed of the truck, while I waved to Erin. Derek walked with her to their car, shaking his head the entire time. *I wonder if he questions my influence on her. I know I would.*

Sliding into the passenger seat of the truck, I clicked my seatbelt into place. Lex hopped in and started the truck. There was no music as we drove down the highway, just the sound of our breathing.

"Lex, are you mad at me?" I asked in concern.

"Just a bit. You're absolutely crazy, do you know that?"

"Yeah, but only around you. I'm sorry, but if I had the chance to do it over, I'd still hit her. What she said...I...it made me so angry."

"I know it did. I think everyone in the bar knows that. Don't fight my battles for me, okay? I need you to fight them with me, and if that means us walking away, then that's what we'll do. Just don't hit anyone else. Okay?"

"Okay."

The gravel crunched beneath the tires of the truck as Lex put it into park in front of the house. Hopping out of the truck, I took a few steps before turning my eyes upward. Thousands of stars filled the Alabama night sky. Some were so big and bright it was as though I could pick them from the sky with my fingers. Suddenly, long arms wrapped around my waist. Looking over my shoulder, I saw Lex looking up toward the stars.

"It's so beautiful," I admitted.

"She is." Lex replied, leaning down and gently placing a kiss behind my ear.

"I meant the stars."

"I know what you meant, but that's not what I meant. The stars got nothing on you."

Giggling, I shook my head. "You and your pick-up lines."

"That wasn't a pick-up line. I'm just being honest. You're beautiful. I wish you could see yourself through my eyes. You'd be in awe."

My heart tripped over itself so many times, it was still somersaulting as we walked through the front door. Telling me he loves me, we carefully made our way up the stairs.

If this is what love really feels like, I never want it to stop. Lex looked over his shoulders as we walked up the stairs to the bedroom. *If the smile on his face is any indication of what's to come, this might just be the best night yet.*

Chapter

Eighteen

The pounding in my dream continued to get louder. It took me a minute to realize the sound was not in my dreams. Rolling over, I gently shook Lex's shoulder. "Babe, I think someone is at the door."

BANG! BANG! BANG! The sound reverberated through the house. Whoever it was seemed relentless. "Lex, the door." I mumbled

"Morning." Sitting up, Lex rubbed his hands over his face as his eyes adjusted to the light coming in from the far window.

"Morning. There's someone at the door."

BANG! BANG! BANG!

"Shit! What time is it?" he asked.

Glancing at the clock beside the bed, I rattled off the time as I buried myself back under the covers. "It's just after eight. Why are they up this early?"

"I love you, but it's Sunday. It ain't that early."

"It is for me. Can you go make them stop?" I whined.

"Yes ma'am." Lex stood and pulled on a pair of gray shorts. My eyes followed his every move as he got dressed and left the room. The first time I woke up and found him lying naked beside me I was little shocked. While I enjoyed the view, it was the first time I had witnessed someone sleeping nude. I'm used to it now, and the view is still incredible.

The idea of staying in bed rolled around in my head a few times, but my curiosity got the best of me. After slipping on a pair of plaid shorts, I straightened my t-shirt and threw my hair up in a messy knot at the top of my head. *I don't have a bra on but I have shorts on, that should count for something since I haven't even had my coffee yet.*

I could hear Lex talking with someone as my feet hit the last stair. He was standing in the kitchen, pouring himself a cup of coffee, when his eyes fell on me. Reaching for my hand, he pulled me towards him. The first thing I noticed about our guest in the kitchen was the gun on his right hip pocket. The second was the gold badge pinned to his chest.

"Indie, this is Jim Strickland. He's an officer with the Lauderdale County Police Department. He's looking for Logan, but from what I understand, he has a couple of questions for us as well. You want some coffee?"

Nodding my head, I took a seat on one of the stools by the counter. "Coffee would be great, thanks."

"Sure thing." I couldn't help but notice the worried look on his face as he handed me my cup of coffee. Lex didn't sit down. Instead, he stood behind me sipping his coffee, with his free hand gripping mine. "Like I said, if I can help you with something, I'll gladly do it," Lex reiterated to the officer.

"Truth is, I was hoping to catch you both. After speaking with Ray and a couple of regulars from the bar, I think it's best I ask you a couple questions first. Now, since I already spoke with your brother, this is just a formality, of course."

Lex's grip tightened on my hand, causing the bones in my fingers to press against one another. "Just get on with it."

Clearing his throat, Jim took a pencil, along with a small notepad, out of his front shirt pocket. "It's my understanding that you are both familiar with a Janet Clark. Ray tells me you all might have had some ill will towards her. Now, I don't see that being the case here, but I'm just covering my bases. I'll know more once I hear back from the department."

"She was my brother's ex-wife. She's got a drinking problem and she likes to blame me for it. What did she do?" he replied, his voice laced with deep concern.

The officer made a couple notes before turning to me, "What about you, ma'am? Did you have any discrepancies with her?"

Squeezing Lex's fingers, I watched as Jim placed the tip of his pencil to the notepad. "I've only met her a few times and each time she was drunk. Each time we saw her, she accosted us. Fortunately, I have no problem defending myself. Last night at the bar, she pushed me while yelling drunken slurs. I responded by knocking her flat on her ass. It wasn't my finest moment as a human being, but one can only take so much," I explained honestly.

Nodding his head, Jim set his pencil down, looking Lex squarely in the eyes. "Did either of you speak with her any time after the incident in the bar?"

"No. We are honestly trying to forget her. What's the point of all of this?" Lex asked, scrubbing his face with his hands before leaning against the counter.

"I'm sorry to be the one to tell you this, but Ms. Clark was in a severe car accident early this morning, around four o'clock. It looks like she might have slammed into a guardrail before hitting a tree head on. She didn't make it. There were open bottles in the backseat, but from the looks of it, some were days old."

"Holy shit," Lex whispered, stumbling back from the counter. Quickly reaching out for him, I grabbed his hand, steadying him on his feet. I could see the guilt already forming in his eyes. *He's going to blame himself for this, and I'm not going to be able to stop it.*

"Is there anything we can do?" I asked. *I was never a fan of hers, but if she has family or something maybe they'll need help.*

"If I need anything more from you, I'll let you know." Nodding his head, Jim walked out the door, closing it quietly behind him. Looking to my right I could see Lex, still frozen in shock, standing in the middle of the kitchen.

"Lex, I love you. This isn't your fault. I can see it in your eyes, and I need you to hear me." *No response.* Reaching up on my toes, I gently placed a kiss on his neck. "I know you've gone somewhere else right now, but I need to know you hear me."

Deep blue eyes suddenly met mine. Raking his hand through his messy brown hair, he held his other hand out from me. At that moment, nothing could keep me from him. My body pulled to him like a magnet as I moved across the floor. "I hear you. I'll admit I'm a little stunned, but I'm okay. Logan is probably going to need me later though, but right now all I need is you. This is a lot to process."

"Okay. What do you want me to do, babe?" I asked.

"Absolutely nothing. I'm going to go back upstairs, where the world is still the same world from yesterday." Softly grasping my hand in his, Lex led me to our bedroom.

Without saying a word he slid into our bed. Taking me with him, he wrapped us under a blanket. I leaned against the headboard as he laid his head in my lap. His long legs surpassed mine, even when he was curled up in my lap. *It must be a funny sight to see such a tall man with such a short woman.*

"Did I ever tell you about my momma?" he asked.

Twirling his brown locks around my finger, I gently stroked his arm with my free hand. "Not really. You mentioned the mirror, but that was it."

"Shit, I got in a lot of trouble over that damn thing." Chuckling to himself, he nuzzled his face against my thigh. "My momma was a stubborn woman. She was always right, and no one could tell her otherwise. She was strong, independent, and fearless. She never took no for an answer and she loved fiercely."

"She sounds wonderful," I admitted sincerely.

"She was. When I was younger all I wanted to do was fall in love with a girl who was just as stubborn and just as fierce. Since the accident all I have thought about was Logan. I wanted to fix what I had done. I wanted to take it back—but I couldn't. Then you came along. All of sudden it was like I could see again. My focus changed."

"I didn't do anything, Lex. I hold no magical force or power."

"You're wrong. You saved me and now you're doing it again. You don't see it do you?"

"Nope. All I see is you. I love you."

"City girl, you make me crazy and that's exactly what I need. Where do you see us in the future?"

"Lex—"

"Just be honest. There's no wrong answer."

Taking a deep breath, I thought about where we could be in the future. "I'm with you. That's where I see us. If you want a family, though—if that's what you're hinting at…I'm not sure I can give that to you. I never pictured myself falling in love like this, let alone starting a family. Maybe one day, but not now. I just can't be responsible for someone else's life."

"A family is a big jump. I just want you. Is that possible—can I have just you?"

"That's a stupid question. Of course you can." My heart skipped a beat as Lex placed a kiss on the outside of my thigh. *Before he runs with whatever idea he's concocting in that gorgeous head of his, I need to make sure he's going to be okay.* "Lex, I'm going to ask you to do something. I know you said no before, but I think with everything that happened last night and everything that will happen tomorrow, it might really help."

"I'm not going to therapy."

"Please? Just go once…you might like it. You need someone to talk to, someone who can help you process all of this."

"I have you."

"That's not what I meant."

"Fine. I'll go on one condition."

Pinching the bridge of my nose, I let out a sigh. "What condition?"

"You go with me."

"Deal."

Rolling over, Lex flashed me a great big grin as he tucked his hands behind his head. "That's good, because I have an appointment on Tuesday at noon. You can come to that one."

"Wait—what?" I asked in shock.

"I thought about what you said and I was talking it over with Logan. He was kind of pissed that I listened to you and not to him. He's been trying to get me to go for years. If it will help me move on from my past, and move on with my life with you, then it's worth a shot."

"I don't know if I should be mad at you right now, or happy. Consider me happyish with a side of angryish."

"Whatever it is, it's cuteish."

"Lex—"

"Yeah, baby."

"I'm not your baby—I'm not anyone's baby. You're starting to get cocky again and it's beginning to annoy me."

"I know I don't own you, I just like getting you all riled up. Besides, I'm only this way with you."

Fuck him and his 'only with you' bullshit. He says it just to get under my skin.

We spent the next few hours lying in bed. He called his brother a few times, but Logan just wanted some time to himself. I couldn't imagine what it must feel like to be him. I wouldn't know whether to be sad, angry, or happy that she was finally gone.

Erin called me a few times, trying to get details from me, but I was lucky enough to be able to dodge most of her questions. Lex took my phone from me the last time she called and put it on mute. He swore if anyone else called, he would start charging them by the minute to talk to me. I asked him if that would make him my pimp. According to him, he's more of an agent, fielding my calls, and Erin was the paparazzi we were trying to avoid. He earned a hard eye roll from me on that one.

Chapter

Nineteen

The sun kept peeking in between the curtains. *Maybe if I position the pillows just right, I can completely block out the light.* I felt Lex get up earlier this morning, but I continued to lie in bed with my eyes tightly shut. It's the first full day-off we've both had, where neither of us had anything scheduled, in over a month. I have no clue why he felt the need to wake up so early, but I wasn't joining him.

All my things are finally unpacked and everything is in its proper place. I apologized profusely to my landlord when I broke the news of my move, but she didn't seem to mind. She told me I had given her a reason to finally let go of it. The week after I moved out, she put it up for sale.

From where I lie, I could hear Lex moving around downstairs. What sounded like chairs scooting across the kitchen floor, followed by a rather loud thud, got my attention. Stretching my arms above my head I twisted and straightened every muscle in my back before sitting up and pushing the covers off my legs. I was rubbing my hands over my face as Lex walked up the stairs. He paused outside of our door for a minute before walking in and sitting on the end of our bed. I couldn't do anything but stare at the grinning lunatic sitting at my feet.

Breaking the silence, I said, "You're up."

"I am."

"You showered and you got dressed."

"I did."

"Why?" I asked in confusion.

"Because I had to. I have something for you."

"Do I need to shower or get dressed?"

"Eventually, but only to keep down the pollution levels. Right now I want to show you something."

Perkiness is overrated. I thought to myself. Just as Lex opened his mouth to say something, I heard a small bark. *What the hell?* "Was that a dog?"

"Before you say anything, I want you to know that I love you. Everything you've given me has been incredible. You showed me how to move on from my past and you've given me a life to look forward to."

THUMP! THUMP! Why is my heart beating so frantically? As I watched Lex walk back toward the door, I heard another little bark. Reaching down, he picked something up in his arms. From the looks of it, it appeared to be quite tiny. As he turned around my mouth fell open in complete disbelief. There, in his arms, was a small black puppy.

Oh my God! "You got me a puppy!" I screeched!

"Yeah. Here, you hold him. His name is on the collar."

I squealed with excitement as the chubby ball of black fur was laid in my lap. "He's adorable!" Picking him up, I sweetly kissed him on the nose. "Aren't you adorable?" I asked. Lifting his head, I turned his collar over to read his name. "Baby?" I questioned, glancing at Lex.

"There's more. Look at the top of the collar," he replied in a cryptic tone.

Holding the puppy tightly in one arm, my fingers slid up the band of the collar until they found a hard piece of metal shaped like a ring. *THUMP! THUMP! THUMP!* My heart was ringing in my ears as I set the puppy back down in my lap. A small silver band was tied to the collar with a thin white ribbon. In the center of the band was a small princess cut diamond.

"Lex—"

"Wait—hear me out. I have this all planned. Do you remember a few months ago when we were talking about kids? Neither of us were ready for that and we weren't sure when we would be. I love you so much and I would give anything to have you as my wife and to watch your belly grow with our baby inside, but I know how much it frightens you. So, I thought we'd do it a little bit differently. Meet Baby. He's ours to spoil rotten and to love endlessly."

"He's perfect," I replied, lightly tracing the one solid white spot on his side. He spun to chase my finger, but tumbled over the blanket. Giggling, I looked over at Lex who was now slipping the ring off Baby's collar.

"Indigo Bryant, I fell in love with you the night I slipped your ballet slipper back on your foot. That night my nightmares were replaced with dreams of you. You make everything so much better––more better. Better than I could ever have imagined. Will you be my wife?"

A tear slipped from the corner of my eyes. *This gorgeous man in front of me is crazy in love with me. My heart has never felt so full.* "Yes. Yes—I'll marry you," I stammered.

Lex reached down and carefully moved the puppy before tackling me. His body engulfed mine and I squealed with laughter beneath him. Rolling over, he pulled me toward him as he slipped the ring on my finger. "You are now the future Mrs. Clark."

"That makes me sound old."

"No, it sounds perfect."

Rolling my eyes, I leaned in and kissed him softly on his lips. "I love you."

"I know. Now get up and get dressed. We have shopping to do. Erin and Derek are coming over later. I'm going to grill us a magnificent feast."

"Does this feast consist of semi-burnt hamburgers and hotdogs?"

"Don't judge me, city girl. I am Lex. Lex is man. Man makes fire," he replied in his best caveman voice.

Laughing, I fell back onto the pillows behind me. "Fire with the help of lighter fluid does not count." I laughed even harder when Lex tossed a pillow at my head and missed. "You're so cocky."

"Only with you," he replied. Pushing himself off the bed, he headed downstairs and left me to get ready for the day. I used to think he was lying when he said things like that, but now that I have seen him around other people, I know it's only with me. He's constantly questioning himself when he's working with Logan or when he's with his friends, but with me he's always so sure of himself.

A small yip beside me, and the touch of a wet nose against my arm, reminded me that I wasn't alone in the bed anymore. Carefully picking up the puppy, I set him on the floor. Rummaging through our closet for a few minutes, I finally grabbed a pair of jeans and an old Green Day t-shirt. Baby followed me as I walked around the room and into the bathroom. As I stepped into the shower he began to cry…and he wasn't giving up. I opened the curtain a few times to peek at him and he instantly stopped, but as soon as the curtain closed he would start whining again.

If this is what a puppy does, I can't imagine what an actual baby would do. The puppy was definitely a better choice for us right now. After wringing out most of my hair, I grabbed a towel off the shelf and stepped out of the shower. Baby was right at my feet barking and pouncing on my toes as I walked back into our room to get dressed.

"Stop it. Let me get dressed first; then we can go outside and run around. I'm sure there will be a ton of sticks for you to chew on." Baby responded with a simple bark as I began to get dressed. Once I began drying my hair, the whining resumed. After I was done, I picked him up and he instantly became silent. Keeping him tucked tightly under my arm, I walked down the stairs to find Logan and Lex in the kitchen.

"You don't have to carry the dog. Put him down, he can walk."

"No, Lex, you don't understand. All he does is bark or whine, but when I touch him he stops. Watch." Bending down, I set Baby down on the ground and he immediately started pawing at my feet and crying. Logan and Lex both stared at me in disbelief.

"Maybe he just wants to go outside. I'll take him." Lex picked Baby up, but the puppy wanted nothing to do with him. He was squirming and whining so incessantly it almost sounded like he was howling.

"What did you do to him? Give him back to me!" Taking the puppy from Lex's arms, I held him against my chest, softly petting the bridge of his nose. Baby immediately calmed down without one hint of a whimper.

"How on Earth have you spoiled that dog in the matter of an hour?" he asked in shock.

"I didn't do anything. He just kept crying, so I picked him up."

"Indie, did Lex explain to you that it is a puppy…it's not a baby."

Glaring at Logan, I shifted the dog in my arms. "He is a baby—that's his name. I don't want to hear him cry, and if he stops when I hold him, then that's what I'm going to do. No one asked for your opinion, Logan, so you can just shut it," I retorted.

As I walked out of the kitchen and through the side door, I heard Logan whisper to Lex, "That's a black lab she's holding. I'd like to see her carry him around when he's full grown. That will be a feat."

"Aww, Logan, are you jealous? If you want, I'm sure Lex would be willing to carry you around. We could even buy you a pretty collar. Maybe something that glitters?" I didn't wait for a response. Instead, I set the puppy down on the grass and watched as he attempted to run. He stumbled and tripped over himself a few times before he got the feel for the grass beneath him. I ended up spending most of the day outside with Baby. We even took a small nap in the hammock by the back deck.

It was almost six o'clock by the time Erin and Derek arrived. I could hear Olivia squealing before I even saw her. She must've caught sight of me when they pulled up. Stepping off the deck, I walked around the house, toward the barn, to find Olivia running full speed at me. Scooping her up in my arms, I covered her tiny face in kisses. "I swear she was just barely walking the last time she was over. Now she's conquering every flat surface."

Laughing, Erin shifted the diaper bag on her shoulder. "That's what babies do, Indie. They grow up."

"Yeah, well, I don't like it." Giving Olivia one more kiss, I set her on the ground before grabbing Erin's hand. "You have to come with me right now. You've got to see this."

Baby made his presence known before we even got around to the back of the house. Poor Lex was trying to calm him down as he sat on the deck barking and whining, while pawing at the screen door. Walking over to Lex, I kissed him on the cheek and picked Baby up to show Erin the surprise Lex had given me.

"Lex got me a puppy. His name is Baby."

"He's adorable." Erin scratched the fur behind his ear as she stared at the hand I was holding him with. "What else did he give you?" she asked knowingly.

"Oh, you know—nothing big. It's just an engagement ring," I replied with excitement.

"An engagement ring? That's fucking huge! Nothing big, my ass. I'm so excited for you guys!"

"Eeek! Derek! I get to plan another wedding." Derek's eyes were wide as he stepped out onto the back deck, carrying a tray of food.

"Good luck with that, Indie. She went full lunatic planning ours."

"Don't worry, I'll keep her under control. No one will have to worry about vagina colored dresses or napkins. We're going to keep it low-key, and less pussy colored."

Derek busted out laughing, while Lex stared at us like we had all gone completely insane. "I feel like I'm missing something here," Lex reluctantly stated. "There were people in pink pussy dresses at your wedding?" Lex handed Derek a beer while looking over at Erin, who was now standing angrily with her hands on her hips.

"They weren't pink pussy dresses!" Erin shouted at us. None of us were able to hold our composure as we all started laughing hysterically. Derek was holding his sides, muttering about pink pussies, while Lex and I kept looking at each other and cracking up. "Fuck you, Indie. Just you wait, you'll have crazy shit happen at your wedding too."

"Aww—Erin, don't get upset. If you want to dress up as a vagina and stand in my wedding, I'll let you. Just don't expect anyone else to rock the pussy pink color. That'll be saved just for you."

"Whatever. Be a better hostess and make me a drink."

"Guys, I think we hurt her feelings. Sorry, Erin!" I blew her a kiss as I headed into the house to pour her a glass of wine. *She can pretend to be mad all she wants, but she knows I'm right.*

By the time Derek and Erin left, I was completely exhausted. Lex helped me clean up most of the mess and then we headed to bed.

I was lying in a tank top next to a very naked man when he grabbed my hand and brought it slowly toward his lips.

"I love you, city girl."

"I love you too. Thank you for the puppy. He's perfect.

"He keeps nipping at my toes," he replied, frustration lacing his voice.

"You may want to consider pants. Trust me when I say you don't want him nipping something else."

"He better not!" Jumping up from the bed, Lex quickly pulled on a pair of boxers before climbing back into bed. His arms wrapped around me, while mine wrapped around Baby.

For the first time in my life, I understand what it feels like to have family that loves me. Lex says I saved him, but I think he saved me—maybe just a little, but I'm not telling him that. I'll keep that secret all to myself.

Epilogue

LEX
FOUR YEARS LATER

For the past eight months, I have watched my wife conspire with my brother behind my back. They didn't think I could hear the whispers when I would leave the room or that I could see the way they gave each other knowing looks when I would walk in. I knew they were up to something. This, however, was not what I would have guessed.

My hand slid across the hood and my cock instantly went stiff. *Fuck me.* It was like when I was nineteen again and I couldn't control it. Every time a sexy girl would walk by, my dick would jump. *Fuck me, it's happening again.* However, this time, the sexy girl was my wife.

She was bending over in a pair of daisy dukes, looking through the back window, as her fingers gently traced the stitching on the leather seats. Turning her head, she caught a glimpse of me.

Seeing her bent over like that would get me hard almost anytime, but this time it's different. This time she was bent over the secret that she'd kept from me. She even had it painted the same deep plum color I had on the last one. The paint shimmered in the sunlight. *I don't know how they did it.* Standing, Indie leaned back against the door, crossing her arms over her chest. *She's going to try to challenge me. I can already see her getting ready for a fight.*

Whatever she wants, she can fucking have it, because right now, my wife is leaning against a 1969 Dodge Charger. And it's all mine. I was going to wait until we got inside, but the idea of making her scream in the backseat is sounding better and better.

Music was spilling out of the open windows. I'm not sure who was singing the song, but damn, it hit home for me. The guy was singing about how love is waking up to Monday's with his girl. Everything is so routine, and life can throw some shit, but waking up to his girl is like seeing Heaven for the first time, every time. Even on a Monday morning, she makes his Earth shake. *That's exactly how I feel with Indie.*

"Lex?" The sound of my name rolling off her tongue got me every time. It's like my savior calling me home.

"Yeah?"

With a wicked grin, she asked, "How big is this back seat exactly? What about the seatbelts? Do you think a baby would fit back here…in a car seat?"

"What?" I asked in confusion. "You're not making any sense. Why would you put Baby in a car seat?"

"Lex, do you remember when I told you I wanted to see what would happen when I stopped my birth control a few months ago?"

"Yeah, I do." *Holy shit. She's not—there's no way!*

"Well, our baby happened, and it's going to need a car seat."

"Fuck the riddles, Indie. Are you telling me we're pregnant?"

"Yep."

"I'm going to be a daddy?" I asked, beaming with excitement.

"Yep." She stood there looking at me all innocently, like I should have expected all of this. *It seems so unreal.*

Trying to wrap my brain around everything that I was just told, I could only respond with, "I don't…this is…we're having a baby!" Rushing to her side, I wrapped my arms around her waist, pulling her against me. I spun us around a couple of times until I felt dizzy. "I didn't think things could get better after we got married—but then you found me this car, and now we're having a baby."

"So you're happy?" she asked, her voice laced with concern.

"I'm more than happy. This is so much better than happy. This is more better, nothing beats more better with you."

"Good. I love you."

"I love you too, city girl."

"Eventually you'll have to stop calling me that. I haven't been a city girl in years."

"It doesn't matter. I'll call you whatever you want. I fucking love you so much."

Her giggle was like a sweet violin to my ears when my lips found her neck. *I'm never going to stop loving her. She's my little taste of Heaven, and I'm going to worship her every chance I get.* Suddenly, a wicked thought came to mind. *I might even start with worshiping her in the backseat of my Charger.*

Other Books by Amber Lacie

Shadows & Light: A Love Ever After Series
Books 1 & 2
Available at: Amazon

Eve is a beautiful woman surrounded by her friends and family. In her twenty-six years of life, nothing exciting has ever happened to her. Everything is going perfectly for her. Little does she know, one summer at the beach could change her life forever.

Theron is the son of a cutthroat multi-billionaire business tycoon. He thought he left behind the world his father created, but things change. His only hope at overcoming his past, is finding the one person he lost so very long ago.

When Eve bumps into Theron, their worlds collide. Nothing can prepare them for the instant fireworks and roller coaster ride waiting for them.

When evil starts to surround them, intent on destroying them, Eve runs into trouble.

Can Theron and Eve find Light among the Shadows? Or will evil win?

*****

PRETTY;
Available at: Amazon

After a lifetime of torture from a man set out to destroy her, Andie finally finds herself surviving on her own free of his grasp despite her past still haunting her dreams.

Laith had his own demons to fight, but now he's thriving in Chicago as the owner of City Ink Tattoos.

When Andie and Laith meet their worlds shift as they find strength in each other. Will they be able to build with the pieces of their hearts they have left, or will their love crumble and fall leaving them both completely shattered?

*****

BREATHE
Available at: Amazon

Sometimes love is fated in the stars. You know you are destined for each other. Your souls entwine and you can't imagine your life without them. Sometimes it's found when you're not looking for it. It peeks around the corner when you least expect it, sweeping you off your feet, carrying you off into the sunset. Sometimes, there are a lucky few who get to experience both. I was one of the lucky ones.

ABOUT AMBER LACIE

Website: www.amberlacieauthor.wix.com/author-blog
Twitter: @amber_lacie
Facebook: http://www.facebook.com/amberlacieauthor

You can contact Amber Lacie at amberlacieauthor@gmail.com

Amber Lacie grew up in Chicagoland and now lives in a quaint little town in Northwest Indiana. She has two beautiful children and a husband who worships the ground she walks on (or at least he should). She is an avid reader and coffee drinker. The love of being able to be transported into another world and experience adventures through someone else's imagination has always captured her attention. Now, she is expanding that love into writing and is looking forward to producing many books.

Made in the USA
Monee, IL
02 April 2024

55594947R00164